Is that a gun in his pocket or . . . ?

Jamie Fields can hardly refuse a free vacation. Jobless and broke, the struggling single gal is in need of serious stress relief. Sure, the set up is suspicious—no one gives away a trip to exotic Cuba—complete with 50,000 dollars cash—just for delivering a package. But once Jamie's enjoying sunny beach days and exhilarating tropical nights, she's too happy to care. Especially when she finds herself hotly pursued by a sexy stranger . . .

The McCoy empire is under siege, and Sam Hayes has been tapped to take care of the culprit. Sam knows better than to get involved with his target, but there's something about Jamie that keeps him from simply finishing the job and moving on. Maybe the hard-bodied hitman just can't wrap his mind around the fact that the first woman to set his soul on fire is a common criminal. The only thing Sam can do is keep her close. An easy enough task—if Sam doesn't do something stupid. Like fall in love with the bombshell he was sent to kill . . .

Books by Shady Grace

McCoy's Boys
Beautiful Criminal
Never Give You Up
The Hitman Who Loved Me

Published by Kensington Publishing Corporation

The Hitman Who Loved Me
McCoy's Boys

Shady Grace

LYRICAL PRESS
Kensington Publishing Corp.
www.kensingtonbooks.com

Lyrical Press books are published by
Kensington Publishing Corp. 119 West 40th Street New York, NY 10018

All Kensington titles, imprints, and distributed lines are available at special
quantity discounts for bulk purchases for sales promotion, premiums, fund-
raising, and educational or institutional use.

Special book excerpts or customized printings can also be created to fit
specific needs. For details, write or phone the office of the Kensington
Special Sales Manager:
Kensington Publishing Corp.
119 West 40th Street
New York, NY 10018
Attn. Special Sales Department. Phone: 1-800-221-2647.

Kensington and the K logo Reg. U.S. Pat. & TM Off.
Lyrical Press and the L logo are trademarks of Kensington Publishing Corp.

First Electronic Edition: June 2017
eISBN-13: 978-1-60183-726-4
eISBN-10: 1-60183-726-7

First Print Edition: June 2017
ISBN-13: 978-1-60183-728-8
ISBN-10: 11-60183-728-3

Printed in the United States of America

To my wonderful editor, Jennifer. You've had my back from day one and I love working with you. I hope our relationship continues to flourish with many more books.

Prologue

"Did you hear me, boy? I said, what brings you to my town?"

Sam Hayes grit his teeth and kept his gaze focused forward. *So much for a quiet drink after a hard day*. He had been sitting at the bar in a small town north of Vancouver, minding his own business, when three country hicks strolled in and decided to stand right behind him.

He sipped his tequila in silence and stared at their reflections in the mirror behind the bar. He noted they were in their mid-to-late twenties. Judging by their restless demeanor, sweaty faces, and huge pupils, they were high on something. Worse than that, all three had the greasiest mullets he'd ever seen.

Sam didn't want to turn around, and he sure as hell didn't want to speak to them—especially when the leader's onion breath made him want to puke. Apparently washing hair and brushing teeth wasn't a regular part of their hygiene.

Instinct warned that he should face them. These types would probably stab a man in the back—especially a man with darker skin than their own. But after the day he had, Sam didn't much care what childish antics they had in mind. All he wanted was a quiet drink and the bartender seemed friendly enough. Now, he wasn't so sure he'd made the right choice in coming here.

Eric Clapton's "Tears in Heaven" lilted through the smoky interior.

Two guys got up, pounded the last of their beer, and took off through a side door. A few others decided to stick it out. Sam had a feeling these boys were well known for causing trouble.

The elderly bartender wiped a tall glass, his eyes darting between Sam and the men. He was nervous. Sam noticed his hands shook as he dried that glass, and he felt sorry for the poor fellow. He felt sorry for those boys, too. They probably didn't have much to do other than cause havoc in a town with less than a thousand people.

"I said…what brings you to my—"

"I heard you the first time." He glanced at the bartender and gave a brief nod. Clearly eager to be of some kind of service, the old fellow refilled his shot glace. "Don't worry. I'm just passing through," Sam added. He wanted to reassure the old man that he had no intention of causing trouble. But as he lifted the drink to his lips, one of the boys knocked it from his hand. Tequila spattered everywhere. The bartender jerked back and hit the row of bottles behind him. Sam's shot glass bounced over the wooden counter top and smashed onto the wooden floorboards.

The bartender turned as pale as the whitewash Sam had just finished applying to a lady's shed. The old guy shook his head, perhaps trying to warn him that messing with these boys wasn't a smart idea. Sam didn't care. The bartender had no idea what shit he'd already gone through in his young life.

Sam spun around on his stool and faced the three men. Even outnumbered, he wasn't afraid of them in the slightest. "Are you going to clean up that mess you made?"

The trio shared an amused glance before the leader tipped his head back and let out a thunderous laugh. "Hell no. Are you gonna get out of my town?"

Sam shook his head. These boys didn't seem all that smart. "Like I said, I'm just passing through."

The shorter, heavyset boy looked at his pals. "Then pass through quicker." His beady brown eyes locked on Sam and narrowed. "We don't like strangers around here."

"Well, that's unfortunate. This is the nineties after all. *Strangers* travel all the time." Sam spun back around and smiled at the bartender. "I'll have another shot, please, then I'll leave."

The bartender stood frozen to the spot. His terrified glance shifted from Sam to the leader of the pack. "This young man hasn't caused any trouble, Joseph. Just leave him alone and then he'll be on his way."

"You know what my father will do to you, old man, if you don't listen to me?" Joseph said in a low, threatening voice. "Don't make me call him."

The old man's face turned ashen again. That's when Sam had enough. All he wanted was a drink and now the poor old bartender was being harassed just for providing him service. He stood, handed a bill to the kind man, and faced the boys. "You're a poor excuse of a man to threaten him like that. He's just trying to earn a living like everyone else."

Joseph snorted. "What are you gonna do about it?"

"How about we go outside and find out?"

"Sure. After you," he sneered, gesturing with his hand for Sam to go ahead first.

Sam shook his head. He knew the second he turned his back to them, all three of them would be on him. He took a step back and balled his fists, holding them high to shield his face. The fight was going to happen right here whether the bartender liked it or not.

Joseph was the first to come forward. He was slightly taller than Sam and had long arms. He balled his right fist and struck his arm out. Sam dodged back, giving Joseph's long reach no chance to get close.

One of the other boys grabbed a pool cue from the nearest pool table and held it like a baseball bat. *So this is how it's going to be, eh?* He didn't mind the challenge. As Joseph came at him again, this time with a left hook, Sam bent low and jammed a hard uppercut of his own right into the guy's ribs.

Joseph stumbled back with a growl of pain. His body hunched forward. Sam knew he'd bruised his ribs, and he would be out of the fray for at least another minute while he caught his breath.

The guy holding the pool cue ran at Sam, holding the skinny end of the cue, and swung the thick end right at Sam's ear. Sam sidestepped, ripping the cue from his hand. As he spun his body around, he belted the pool stick across his back with all of his strength. The stick cracked over his back as pieces of wood splintered and scattered across the floor. Sam hurled the guy forward with a boot to his ass.

"Save the Best for Last" by Vanessa Williams hummed pleasantly through the bar as Sam yanked on the hoodie of the third man, jerking him forward, and cracked him in the nose. Blood gushed down the man's lips and chin.

"Fuck!" the guy screamed as Vanessa's beautiful voice carried through the dismal space like a contradiction. Sam never liked that song but the face behind the voice sure had a lovely appeal.

He jerked to the side as a liquor bottle flew past his face and smashed against a wall.

The man with the broken nose apparently gave up and sat at a nearby seat, holding his bloody face, his terrified gaze sweeping through the room. The third man lunged at Sam, spearing him in the stomach. They flew back and collided against the wall right next to a dartboard. Sam cringed as his back banged hard against the wood paneling, but as the guy yanked back to swing up at him, he ripped a dart from the board and jammed it in the guy's shoulder.

"*Ah*! Mother fucker!" He yanked the dart from his flesh and threw it on the floor.

Sam grabbed his bad arm, spun him around, and yanked his arm behind his back. The sharp sound of bone snapping and the guy's ear-splitting scream echoed through the bar as the patrons stared, wide-eyed, still drinking their beer.

Sam shoved the idiot forward and went after Joseph.

The leader of the crew stood there panting, still holding his ribs. He lifted his hand, palm up, and cried, "Please, just stop! We don't want any more trouble."

Sam tipped his head back and let out a rumble of laughter. "Oh, really? I was under the impression that you own this town."

"No. No, sir," Joseph said. "I was just joking." He cringed and lowered his head as Sam walked right up to him, grabbed the collar of his shirt and dragged him to the bar.

"You owe this man an apology."

"I—I'm sorry, Fra-ankie."

The old bartender looked surprised as Joseph begged for forgiveness like a pathetic child.

"And you're going to come back and clean up this mess, aren't you?" Sam added.

Joseph nodded his head fast. "Yes. Yes. I promise. We will. We'll come back."

"Good. Now get the fuck out of here," a sharp, dominant voice cut in. "Punks like you make me sick."

Sam released Joseph and turned toward the commanding tone.

A man wearing a black fedora and matching three-piece suit stood inside the entryway. Two guys who looked close to Sam's age stood on one side while a big bald guy with scars on his face stood on the other. He looked like he'd snap a neck and never blink.

But the man in the suit was the one who commanded Sam's attention. He had a sharp stare, as if he could see all of Sam's secrets. It made him feel as though he stood in the path of a spotlight.

"Mister McCoy," the bartender said in a shaky voice. "I had no idea you'd be in town today. Let me get you your favorite drink."

"That's okay, Frankie. I'm not staying long. We were walking by and heard the commotion. I was beginning to think I'd have to send Benjamin in to finish the job." McCoy turned his attention back to Sam and smiled. "Where did you learn to fight like that, son?"

Sam cleared his throat, embarrassed to admit it, but he didn't want to lie to this man. He dipped his head slightly and looked at the floor. "My aunt."

"Really?" McCoy chuckled. When Sam looked up again, the guys beside McCoy blinked as if in surprise, and the bald guy had yet to have an expression on his ugly face. McCoy ruffled the hair of one of the teenagers. "These are my boys, Terry and Gabriel. We could use a good man like you. How old are you?"

Sam glanced at the bartender and made an apologetic face. It wasn't the old guy's fault that Sam looked like an adult, and it wasn't Sam's fault the guy didn't ask for ID. "Seventeen, sir."

Something gleamed in McCoy's eyes. "And you can fight like that. I'm impressed. Do you know who I am, son?"

Sam narrowed his eyes and looked the man over more thoroughly. He didn't look familiar at all. "No, sir."

"That's all right." The man stepped forward and lifted his hand. Sam noticed every finger had a gold ring on it. "I could offer you the world if you come with me. What do you say?"

Auntie Rose needed money and someone to care for her. The doctor said she needed meds to keep her head clear. Without her love and guidance, Sam knew he'd either be dead or in jail, or maybe wasting his life on drugs. It didn't take much for him to make up his mind.

He looked McCoy straight in the eyes, and shook his hand.

Chapter 1

Sam's eye twitched as another shrieking cry assaulted his nerves. He watched the scene unfold, thinking there wasn't much difference in the hysterical tone from someone knowing their life is about to end, and someone whose life is just beginning.

Screaming babies made him feel funny. Maybe he should do something to stop the deranged hollering, but he wouldn't know what to do other than gently rub a small rosy cheek and hope it didn't break.

Terry McCoy, his brother and best friend, had just become a father for the second time, and his little person was wailing like a demon in the hospital nursery, surrounded by other mini people.

Kids were a whole other language for Sam. He couldn't even remember ever holding one. Even though he thought they were cute and all, he had to admit he was afraid of them. He had been an only child, sent off to be raised by his estranged aunt so Mommy and Daddy could live life like rock stars in the south of France. He knew they loved him in their own way, but responsibility didn't flow willingly in their veins. They needed their freedom, and to some degree he understood that. With age, his resentment dwindled somewhat, yet he still felt awkward when they did decide to pay a visit once or twice a year, instead of the usual birthday and Christmas cards filled with cash.

He didn't want or need their money. All he ever wanted as a kid was to spend time with them, not read the pathetic note on the card about how much they missed him and how they enjoyed traveling.

Auntie Rose did her best to raise him right, though ultimately he became a bit of an oddball like her. She had a perfectly teased afro right out of the seventies and wore thick, green-rimmed glasses. She loved real-life crime books and hairless cats. She put icing sugar in her coffee, and crocheted on the steps of her little trailer while Otis Redding blared through the open windows.

Although Sam thrived on those crime books, he hated cats, and he kept his tight curls neatly trimmed. It was hard enough growing up with light brown skin—he didn't want a crazy afro to go with it. But he couldn't control everything. Three weeks after his fourteenth birthday he smashed up his pedal bike and broke a front tooth. Auntie Rose thought it would be a great idea to replace the missing tooth with a gold one. *"It looks cool, my boy."* Even though he had been teased most of his life about that tooth and told that he might as well become a rapper, he still kept it…for her.

And while he kept his coffee black, he absolutely loved Otis Redding, and sometimes had the notion to sing out loud—as long as he was alone. He'd never win a gig, but he could belt out a few decent notes in the shower.

The little one wiggling in that plastic box sure had a set of lungs on her. She was beautiful and perfect, as every baby should be. He smiled as he watched her wrinkly red face scrunch up for another scream. She had just become a part of a family that would love her to pieces and always protect her. Mary would spoil the girl rotten as she did with their firstborn son. She also had uncles that would kill for her. How he envied everything good she would get in life.

It actually surprised Sam how good of a father Terry had turned out to be, considering his father forced him into a life of crime and made Terry into something he despised. Sam knew that Terry would encourage his kids to be what they wanted to be—not directed around like an employee as Terry had often been treated. Colton McCoy loved his son, but he just didn't see how the life he'd chosen for his family was only what he wanted for himself.

Many years ago, Sam decided that a true blue family was just a label for other people. He knew it the minute he watched Auntie Rose pull out a rifle on those front steps and shoot a groundhog for their dinner that night. She went right back to her crocheting and told Sam to go fetch the furry beast and toss it on her cutting board.

While he was shocked and appalled that she could be so cruel and kill his secret pet, he was more amazed at her precise shot at such a long distance. It didn't take long before Auntie Rose taught him a few things about the darker side of life, and the fact that her glasses were cheaters. She could see just fine.

He learned quickly that he wasn't born to love. He was designed to kill people.

Fate took a turn for him in that bar on a balmy night many years ago. Those degenerates didn't expect to get their asses handed to them by a seventeen-year-old kid. Maybe they didn't like his quiet nature, or the fact that a black man had the nerve to drink in their bar. To their chagrin and broken bones, he'd taken all three of them within three minutes. Fighting came as a second nature to Sam. Not a single person in this world scared him. Well, only one person could command his fear, and that was Colton McCoy, when he was alive. One bad move and Colton could simply nod his head and Sam would've disappeared like all the others. Now that Colton was gone, Sam had nobody to fill that void. Sometimes he wondered if that made him less than human. Most of the time, he didn't much care.

He remembered like it was yesterday how the older fella looked like a teamster. Colton McCoy had taken Sam under his wing and treated him like a son—as he had done with Gabe. Ben, the brawny man with the scars, had become Sam's mentor. He taught Sam everything he knew. When age and too many broken bones over the years caught up to Ben and he wasn't able to take on as many tasks, Sam became the gunman for the empire. It came as a bitter surprise to them all when, out of jealousy, Ben tried to kill Terry in the mountains. Apparently Ben hated becoming Colton's right hand at home, even though he could've chosen to walk away with his chin held high, not forced to wait on Colton like a butler. In some ways Sam understood Ben's resentment, but Terry didn't deserve the bullet from Ben's gun. Terry was just the son of a crime boss and never wanted that life anyway. Targeting Terry had been a huge mistake. Ben may have been Sam's mentor, but Terry was Sam's brother in all the ways that mattered.

In a short matter of time, Gabe and Terry had become Sam's best friends, and now that Colton was gone, things had changed. Terry never wanted what Colton created for him, and Sam thought his adopted brother made the right choice giving it all up. He never could've left the business while his father was still alive. Colton needed his son by his side, especially after losing his first wife—Terry's mother.

Terry looked happier now and Sam envied the change in his brother's life. They all knew it would end one day, and luckily it ended well for Terry and Gabe. Sam didn't hold that much confidence for his final chapter of life.

His brothers had it all, and Sam envied their happiness. He didn't mind being left behind, because somebody had to toe the line.

Sam wouldn't change his past for anything for the world, because he wouldn't be the man he was today without all of it—even the bad shit.

His uncommitted glance wandered to the sexy little nurse on the other side of the glass. She made her way to each little plastic basket to check on the little devils. They didn't seem to care for her attention. They waved their little fists in the air, wanting nothing else but a tit to suck on. Hell, so did he.

Sam released a deep breath and fogged the glass in front of his face. As the little ginger nurse glanced up, he drew a smiley face with his fingertip. Instead of a pretty grin he had hoped to see, the nurse glared, shook her head, and turned her back to him.

Huh. He raised a brow. Since when did people have to be so serious in a hospital? People were dying all over the place and this nurse, surrounded by new life, couldn't even smile at his smiley face.

He checked his watch. In about ten minutes he'd have a tidy seventy-five grand wired to his account in the same small town where he'd first met Colton McCoy and his boys. Sam needed the money badly from all the bills he'd accumulated with his aunt's medication and her overall well-being. She thought the money deposited into her account twice a month was from the government, or sometimes from lottery tickets she never bought, and that suited him just fine. To Sam, Auntie Rose was his mother, and he'd take care of her until the day she died—no matter how dead tired or broke he'd become in the process.

He was confident the job would go smoothly today as long as Mary didn't get wind of it. She didn't need to know he was about to inject a very powerful and newly designed poison that was virtually untraceable, into a man in the next ward. Mary would be devastated and disgusted with him if she knew Sam didn't really come here to coddle the baby and wish them congrats. He was a man, dammit, and he had work to do. Despite being happy for Terry and Gabe's drastic change in routine, to Sam, his life could never be truly normal—not when he lived by a steady aim.

"Isn't she beautiful?" a familiar voice murmured behind him.

Sam shrugged before he turned to face Terry, second time father of less than an hour. The guy looked ridiculously happy and Sam felt a twinge of jealousy. "She seems a little fat," he answered truthfully.

Terry's eyes widened in shock for a second before he laughed and playfully slugged Sam's shoulder. "Almost ten pounds, my little angel. That's a healthy baby girl right there."

Sam grimaced, not by the hit to his shoulder, but imagining the last bag of potatoes he'd bought. *How could something that big break out of a woman's cooch?* That couldn't be normal. He forced the scary thought from his mind and glanced back again at the curvy little nurse. She had a shapely bum that appealed to his basic instincts. It didn't even matter how she'd glared at him only a moment before. Angry sex had its rewards.

"Hello?"

He blinked as Terry snapped his fingers, and Sam suddenly remembered he'd said something. "Sorry, bud." He shifted on his feet and jammed his hands into his pockets. "What do you call her?"

"No name yet—"

"How about President's Choice?" Sam hollered with laughter as Terry's eyes gaped in shock.

Sam's laughter curbed as a baby shrieked. He regarded Terry more seriously, or at least tried to be sincere. "How's Mary doing?"

Terry glanced at the nurse then Sam, and raised a brow. "Exhausted, but in really good spirits. Just think, you're next in line for all this splendor."

Gabe's life had changed the moment he'd crashed his Cessna into the Canadian Rockies. Thankfully, Mima lived up in that remote terrain and happened to be out with her sled dogs when she came upon the crash. Their crazy story started while Gabe healed in Mima's cabin, and then Ben and his crew came after them for the stash of cocaine in Gabe's plane. Sam chuckled out loud. That right there is pure romance.

And Terry, well, he couldn't help but return to the boonies when he met Mima's friend Mary. Knowing Terry, he probably fell into insta-love with the woman before he even banged her. When Colton was murdered by his second wife, Terry rushed back to fulfill his duty of running the empire. But when Mary came after him and was subsequently kidnapped, Terry jumped right into his role as the big boss that he hated and did everything to get her back.

"Pfft." Sam shook his head, imagining Terry's living room carpet covered with squeaky toys, while god-awful curtains hung from the windows. "I'll leave the 'happy wife—happy life' bullshit to you guys." His gaze followed the nurse's round bum again. There were times in his life when he'd wanted a relationship, but his line of work always put a damper on things. A good woman deserved more than a brief fling with a non-committed man, which was why hookers and strippers were his main course these days. Many of them didn't want a commitment anyway. They lived life in the fast lane to how it suited them—in the moment—not for anyone else. He couldn't promise to return home any given night, or to give a woman his heart. His heart didn't even know what love meant.

Sam released a dejected sigh. He liked good girls, but they were on a whole other level than he could ever reach.

"When was the last time you went on a real date? A real date with a broad that shouldn't be institutionalized, or paid."

Sam frowned as he thought about it for a moment. "There was nothing wrong with Annie."

Terry roared with laughter. "She painted her toenails five times a day all different colors."

Sam shrugged. "She had cute feet, so what? Plus they glowed under the black lights in the club."

"Didn't she try to paint yours one day?"

He ignored that question. If Sam admitted that on one exciting night he had blue nail polish on one side and green on the other, Terry would never leave him alone and probably tell everyone about it. But he couldn't refuse Annie. She had a smile that could undo the stitches on his gitch.

"And what about that skinny brunette from last year? Didn't she think you were a chocolate bar salesman? Hmm? She was that dumb to believe you just because you brought her a chocolate bar every night."

A slow smile curved Sam's mouth. "Yeah, Rhonda. She did all kinds of things in return for that chocolate."

"Holy fuck you're a twat." It was then that Terry angled his head and frowned, as if only now realizing an important detail. "Didn't I just call you a few minutes ago? How did you get here so fast?"

Sam gripped Terry's shoulder, forcing him to wander down the hall, far away from the miniature choir behind them. His ears were about to bleed. "I happened to be close by is all."

Terry halted in the pale blue and pink hallway. He leaned closer and whispered fiercely, "Are you here on a job?"

When Sam didn't answer immediately, Terry pulled back and thrust a hand through his neglected hair. "Seriously? You're here"—he pointed to the floor between them—"you're *here* working, aren't you? In this hospital? Do you have no couth at all?"

Terry's reddening face contradicted the cheery pink and blue pastel walls behind him. Sam gave him a look to shut him up. "I haven't had a proper vacation in years, thanks to you. I have to pay for it somehow. Besides, it's just a quick job, nothing major."

"My newborn daughter is down the hall."

The wild fatherly look in Terry's eyes made Sam lean back slightly, thinking they may come to blows in the newborn ward. "How was I supposed to know Mary would deliver today? I don't know how that shit works." He sighed, forcing himself not to lose his temper in this place scented with baby powder. "The guy is in the next ward anyway. What's the big deal?"

Terry glanced down each end of the hallway and gripped the shoulder of Sam's shirt, yanking him toward a quiet corner. "What if something goes wrong? How do I explain to Mary that Uncle Sammy just snuffed-out a man in intensive care?"

Unruffled by Terry's hard grip, Sam patted his shoulder and smiled. "I'm sure you'll think of something, buddy. You know how it is."

Terry blew out a frustrated breath. "Fine. There's no use talking to you. You're worse than a woman."

Sam chuckled. "Don't let Mary hear you say that," he teased.

When Terry glared at him, Sam grinned and brushed past to head down the hall toward the next ward. He paused a few yards down the hallway and glanced over his shoulder. "I'll send flowers. Carnations, right?"

The anger dissipated in Terry's eyes. Everyone knew carnations were his mom's favorite, and now, Terry bought them for Mary. Sam's heart almost tripped as a slow smile crossed Terry's face. The sucker caved so easily.

"I'm leaving for my vacation this afternoon. Don't call me unless somebody's dying." He strolled away before Terry could argue that point. This would be Sam's first real vacation without the task of having to kill somebody, or constantly check over his shoulder. He needed it more than Terry could ever understand.

As he headed toward the ICU, he spotted a male nurse nearing an unmarked door. "Excuse me, nurse?"

The young man had just swiped his card and turned the knob to open the door. "Yes. Can I help you?"

Sam discreetly scanned the hallway. When he was sure nobody else lingered nearby, he feigned an expression of desperation and walked right up to him. "My aunt—I don't know what's wrong with her."

Before the nurse could react, Sam shoved him through the door, which led into a small supply room. He shut the door behind them, and with a quiet apology, he covered the man's mouth with one hand and gripped the pressure point on his neck with the other. As the nurse slunk against the wall, Sam gently eased him down to a sitting position. He removed the nurse's white coat from over his scrubs and quickly put it on.

Sam checked his watch. He was right on the mark for shift change. Quickly, he transferred the syringe from his inside pocket to the outer pocket of the white coat. With Auntie Rose in mind, he slipped on a smart-looking pair of reading glasses and exited the supply room. With an air of authority, he headed toward the room where a police officer stood guard.

With shift change creating a perfect diversion, the officer thought nothing suspicious of Sam and nodded his head as he brushed past to enter the room. But to his surprise, Sam wasn't alone.

A woman sat in silent misery at the bedside, her dainty white hands clinging to the left hand of the unconscious man. He noted the massive wedding set on her finger, the expensive white pantsuit and huge diamond earrings. It wasn't his money she flaunted, it was hers. She was a rich girl and he was her husband.

The man who'd betrayed her.

The man her father hired Sam to kill.

Without saying a word, she looked up from her husband's pale face and stared at Sam. Her eyes said more than words could ever express. Hope and faith. Maybe it was misguided, but it was there. He felt it as if she'd said the words. Sam knew immediately she was the type who would forgive her husband for anything and everything he had done in this world. But what she probably didn't know was that she wasn't his one and only love. He had been living a double life for the past fifteen years and he was planning to use drastic measures and collect on her hefty life insurance. He didn't even have a job because little wifey had tons of money. This husband whom she loved, had children with another woman. And if that wasn't enough of a blow, the fact that he had hired a man to kill her, and take her away from the children she had given him, was enough reason for Sam to enjoy this particular job.

Thankfully, her father discovered his son-in-law's little secret by chance one day as he headed out to view a new investment property. Recognizing his daughter's luxury car which had a one-of-a-kind paint job, the father pulled over and parked beside the curb. But before he could open his door, a man and a woman stepped out of a cozy restaurant, hand-in-hand, and got into his baby's car. The other woman was young and beautiful. Seeing them together had put a tear into the old man's eye. It was in that painful, enraging moment when he decided to hire a private investigator. Each week as new details emerged about the cheating husband and then his ultimate goal, the father took quick action. He called a friend, who called another friend, until way down the line Sam got a call.

Sam smiled while inserting the tip of the syringe into the IV, and felt better about the poor woman. She'd survive this mess. She'd move on with her life, and maybe, just maybe, find a good man she could trust.

Luckily for Sam, the idiot husband got himself into a bit of a bender and smashed up his car, hence the officer sitting outside. Even with the law right on his hip, Sam felt confident that he'd pull this off without a snag. It was Sam's choice to do it this way, rather than the crazy, and dangerous, stand-off the father wanted to see. They were in a hospital after all, a convenient, safe place for this man to die. They could transfer him straight down to the morgue with relative ease.

"This will help with the pain," Sam offered, thinking of her— not her husband.

With tears in her eyes, she nodded and looked back at her husband's face.

Having no time to waste before the heart monitor would skip into a frenzy, Sam dropped the empty syringe back into his pocket and exited the room without looking back.

But as luck would have it on this beautiful autumn day, as he neared the end of the hallway, he heard a commotion. "That's him!" a man shouted.

Without thinking, he glanced over his shoulder and made eye contact with the officer. Exactly what he should never do. Ben had taught him years ago to never make eye contact with anybody of authority when you just killed somebody. He cursed himself for being careless over such an easy job. The male nurse had woken up sooner than he'd thought and was already standing next to the police officer and pointing right at Sam. As the officer shouted orders into his radio, Sam darted around the corner and made an insane dash to the nearest stairwell.

The warning beeper to his victim's heart monitor started shrieking through the ward. The doctor raced into the room, followed by his team of nurses.

Fuck.

Sam whipped open the door leading into the stairwell on the north side of the building and took a chance by jumping down three steps at a time. *This would not be a good time to break your ankle and get caught. Think about the perfect record.* He'd reached the main floor landing in rapid time when he heard shouting on the stairs above.

He ripped off the white coat and flung it on the floor. As he adjusted his shirtsleeves and took a deep breath, he thought of what Auntie Rose would say at a time like this. She'd cluck her tongue at him then say, *"The world is yours, my boy. Take it by the hairy balls."* How he loved her frank manner of speech.

He pushed through the door, immediately eyeing three security guards taking up post in front of the lobby doors. All eyes trained on him as their radios screeched with the report.

Sam's muscles tightened in preparation as he released a steady breath. The three men in uniform focused on him. The second they took a step forward with hands on holsters, Sam shot off like the devil toward the emergency ward. As he reached a row of wheelchairs lined up on the far wall, he grabbed one and shoved it behind him. The chair violently wheeled toward the officers like a good guard dog, and smashed into the knees of one of the guards, making him tumble over it and crash to the tile floor.

A woman screamed.

"Hey!" a man shouted. "Stop him!"

Sam burst through the emergency doors beneath the overhang in the back, nearly taking down a man struggling on his crutches. "Asshole!" the guy shouted, wielding a crutch in the air.

Police sirens shrieked as he ran past a parked ambulance and darted into the busy street. The two remaining guards were hot on his heels, but the bigger man had already begun to struggle and wheeze.

A car honked and screeched to a halt as Sam jumped up and slid on his ass over the hood. He got his advantage as the guards were suddenly halted in between the flow of traffic in the middle of the street.

He cut through the nearest alley and didn't slow down. Despite years of smoking and his lungs screaming to stop and rest, Sam wouldn't give up until his lungs collapsed or one of the officers shot him in the back of the leg.

For some silly reason the only thing rushing through his mind as he turned onto the next sidewalk was that he told Terry he'd send carnations for Mary. What color should he send her, and how many? *What's expected for gifts when you pop out a kid?* It would be unforgivable if he didn't make good on his word. Terry would know something happened—if he didn't already—and give him a blast of shit.

Still, that was a close call. *Too* close.

As he caught his caving breath, he scanned the street and spotted a bargain clothing store a few shops down. He rushed in, grabbed a pair of jeans off a shelf, a hoodie from a rack, and went straight to a dressing room. Once he transferred his wallet and cigarettes into his pockets, and removed the reading glasses, he stepped out of the dressing room like a new man.

"Ah, just what I need." With calm only a man used to a life of chaos could have, he strolled over to a row of baseball caps and fitted the nearest one onto his head.

The cashier stared at him with wide, unbelieving eyes, before her nervous gaze shifted to the street. Two hospital guards and a few cops stood outside hitting up pedestrians for information.

Sam smiled at the girl. She looked barely of age, probably only in the work force for a few months. He'd bet a grand she was about to pee behind that counter.

He lifted his hands to reassure he didn't have a weapon. "You have nothing to fear from me." With one hand still raised, he reached into his pocket with the other, pulled out a few bills and gently placed them onto the counter. "This is more than enough for the clothes, and a little extra for you."

She nodded despite the shimmer of tears in her eyes. "I won't say anything. Just promise you won't hurt me."

Sam smiled again, positive she wouldn't alert the cops. "I promise, and I appreciate your cooperation. It's not what you think."

He knew she didn't believe him. "Whatever you say, mister."

Sam headed toward the front door.

"You—you're gonna go out there? There's cops everywhere," the girl said, her eyes wide with surprise, her mouth curved up in a *do it, I dare you* grin.

Sam couldn't help a low chuckle. She may be scared, but like a typical kid, she was thrilled by the chase. He headed for the door again, but paused to say over his shoulder, "If I were you, I'd treat myself to a night out with that money. It's Saturday, the best day of the week."

The cashier blushed and pocketed all of the money. "We don't have cameras in here. Stuff goes missing all the time." She shrugged, obviously more comfortable now that he was leaving, and maybe because she had made a few bucks for keeping her mouth shut. She grinned. "Have a good day, sir, and good luck."

Sam winked and walked out of the store, right in front of the men in uniform. He knew he wouldn't be recognized with a new outfit and a baseball cap. He plastered an expression of concern on his face. "What's going on?" He stood next to one of the officers, withdrew a cigarette and his lighter from the case. As he lit the end and took a long drag, one of the cops turned to face him.

The officer gave Sam a good once-over and nodded. "We're looking for a man who just escaped from the hospital."

"You mean a *mental* patient?"

The cop shook his head. "No. All we know at this time is that he was wearing grey slacks with a white button-up shirt, glasses, and he looked to be of mixed descent. Average height and build." The cop glanced at him again from shoes to baseball cap.

Sam hid his amusement as he sucked in another deep drag of his cigarette. Mixed descent could mean anyone this day and age. He was often confused as being Asian or Native American, or a mixture of the two, and he enjoyed keeping people guessing his true African-Irish origin. "I see."

Another officer joined them. Sam recognized him as one of the guys connected to the McCoys. They often called upon him for Intel: when patrol would be going by, or to make tickets and profiles disappear, or to dig up background on a person. He was also among the badges at Colton's funeral. As they made eye contact, Sam kept his expression passive. "Well, I hope you find him. We don't need criminals running around these streets."

The second officer didn't bat a lash. "Absolutely. Be sure to contact the police department if you happen to see this man. You can move along now." The cop smirked, nodded his head, and turned the other way.

Sam grinned and headed down the street at a casual pace. As he passed a few vagrants sitting along the edge of the sidewalk, a happy couple walking hand-in-hand, and a few suits rushing to get to work, he wondered what life would be like on their side of the fence. Was a normal life boring or was it peaceful? He halted, turned back, and tossed a few bills into the cups lined up in front of the poor men, then headed back down the street.

Auntie Rose would be proud of him. No matter how tight she was for money, she always did her best to help others who needed it more than she did. Despite her horrible cooking, she regularly volunteered at shelter houses and soup kitchens. She handed out blankets during the winter months, and was even known to haul women back home, even if only for her own company.

She'd be sitting on her front steps right about now, possibly crocheting a scarf or perhaps a pair of socks. He had a closet full of her colorful creations he didn't have the heart or the balls to wear. Sam chuckled out loud remembering the last pair of socks she'd given him, half-yellow and half a putrid, baby-shit green. He put them on in front of her, of course, and she smiled sweetly with open happiness.

"Oh, they look wonderful, sweetheart."

He'd lifted his pant legs and had to force himself not to laugh at his appearance. But the moment he got home he ripped those things off and tossed them into the closet. It wasn't the color that bothered him, or the fact that they were three sizes too big, it was the horrible scratch of the wool on his skin. He'd spent a majority of the night rubbing lotion on his feet and ankles to alleviate the burning.

Never again.

He made it back to his truck and headed to the nearest flower shop. With Mary in mind, and the newest addition to their little family, he chose five-dozen pink carnations and had them delivered to the hospital. He couldn't think of what to write on the card, but as that bag of potatoes came to mind, he quickly scribbled, *I wish you a speedy recovery. Love, Sam.*

After a brief ferry ride and short drive to his quaint apartment downtown, once again he became invisible with the mixture of the homeless, the street thugs, and the junkies. Nobody would ever guess a hired killer to lived here, but while it wasn't the safest or cleanest, or most aromatic place to live, it provided the perfect cover. He had friends who enjoyed a lavish lifestyle, only to eventually cause too much attention to themselves because of it. Sam rarely wore a suit, and he didn't drive the latest sports car. He liked his old Ford pickup just fine, especially when the beast packed a few surprises under that hood.

While he quickly packed some comfortable clothes for his first vacation that was bound to give him privacy and relaxation, Sam realized he wouldn't have time to visit Auntie Rose before his flight.

On impulse, as he'd done many times over the years, he went online and wired some money to her account. It always made him feel good to provide for her. One day he'd take her on a trip with him. But for now, he needed time to himself, without mindless chatter and responsibilities, or the threat of a possible job.

He couldn't wait to get on that plane and head to paradise. A place far away from anyone he knew, and quiet enough to maybe give him some peace. If peace could ever be found for a man like him.

Chapter 2

Over seven months had passed since she'd had the pleasure of a real penis. Jamie Fields watched as rickety old Groundskeeper Jobe ambled across the lawn, and wondered if she should hit him up for a one-night stand. That's how desperate she had become, because she couldn't get anything else.

"Beautiful day, isn't it?" Jobe asked, and waved his liver-spotted hand out in front of him, gesturing toward the trees.

The leaves were beginning to change to the autumn hues of pale yellow and burnt orange in the deep woods of Northern Ontario. This was the time of year that fishermen loathed as the boating season would soon be at an end.

"It sure is," she called back, and released a disgruntled breath as he hobbled away. Ol' Jobe probably got lucky more than she did. He was a horny old man and smooth with the widows that often vacationed here. She shuddered, recalling a time she'd accidentally caught him massaging the back of a woman's neck while whispering something in her ear. That woman looked as if she was about to have an orgasm, and it was extremely uncomfortable to watch.

Jamie glanced across the grounds and sighed. She both loved and hated this time of year. While she loved the beautiful fall colors, the hot days, and cool evenings at the beginning of September, she hated having to leave the wilderness and return to her apartment in the city. One month to go before the fun ended and real life returned.

Back to real life and real problems.

Every May she left home to return to Sharp Ridge Lodge, three hours north of the city—as their housekeeper. While Jamie didn't enjoy the daily routine of cleaning up after people, summer life in the middle of nowhere had many rewards. After supper she could do as she pleased. Swim. Fish.

Hike across the terrain that spanned for miles on end. Go for a leisure boat ride. Sit by a campfire. Have a sauna and jump off the dock. Enjoy a few drinks in the rustic lounge in the main lodge, and play cards with the staff and guests on rainy days. All of these things were a wonderful and relaxing experience, and she met hundreds of people throughout the season.

Sharp Ridge Lodge was famous for its rustic setting and world-class fishing. It came as no surprise to staff if a customer returned with a forty-pound pike or a ten-pound pickerel. The guests may be awestruck, overexcited, and eager to bring their prize home, but to everyone who worked here, those catches were just another day in the bush.

In total they had a dozen cabins of various sizes for the guests, neatly situated behind the main lodge which stood on the ridge overlooking the bay. Each of the staff had their own tiny cabin nestled in the back on the hill overlooking the main grounds. Other buildings scattered over the property consisted of a fish cleaning hut, generator and pump house, mechanic shop, laundry building, and a sauna. Sharp Ridge Lodge had everything a person could want for a wilderness retreat. Although the lodge had that rustic, in-the-middle-of-nowhere vibe, guests were still treated with as much luxury as they wanted. All with running water, thanks to a screened hose running from the lake to the pump house, where it snaked off to each cabin underneath the lawn.

But the end of the season was fast approaching. Another group of guests would arrive by plane this afternoon, and next week the last group would arrive. Guest accommodations usually shut down during the last week of September, and the staff would winterize the buildings during the first week of October. In another month Jamie would be back at home, desperately searching for a new winter job.

She eyed the list of guests from her clipboard and which cabin needed preparing before their arrival. One cabin with two queen beds for two elderly couples on a three-week stay; a single honeymoon retreat for two newlyweds for one week; and a single cabin for one man on an indefinite stay.

She stared at the last name, Jack Daniels, and chuckled. That was her last foster father's favorite whiskey. How she missed his funny anecdotes when he got plastered. He had been one of the decent ones. So many homes she had been taken from and dropped off to over her younger years, only to live in fear of either being abused or of liking them too much. Her favorite "father" had died of liver failure when she was seventeen. A year after that his wife passed away after a botched operation, and since then Jamie had been on her own. She'd never known her real parents, only that they had been too young to care for a child, and when too much time had passed without an offer of adoption, the foster system took her into its clutch.

Jamie wouldn't allow herself to love anyone ever again. The good ones always ended up dying, and the bad ones never seemed to learn from their mistakes. More than once she had been sexually abused by an adult who was supposed to care and provide for her—not treat her as a toy or a pet. She'd been beaten to the point of not being able to go to school for risk of bruises being noticed, and she'd gone without a proper meal on many occasions. Those days were hard, but they hardened her as a person. When her final foster folks came into the picture, Jamie was a damaged girl, yet they loved her and provided for her, made her feel like she was a part of a family. When they died, her perfect world had vanished, replaced, once again, by an uncertain future. The only certain thing in Jamie's life now was her resolve to continue pushing forward.

Maybe one day she could make her dream into reality and be loved by somebody who wouldn't leave her behind. Fame and fortune had never been a part of that dream, only the certainty of having a loving home.

Never give up. Never give in.

"Hey."

From her perch on the top of a picnic table, she turned toward the familiar voice and smiled. Monty, the lodge cook, strolled toward her wearing an Iron Maiden T-shirt, a black bandana with skulls imprinted everywhere, and jeans with the knees completely ripped out. What set him off from every other man she'd met over the years was his sense of humor, and a ridiculous porn moustache. Monty was the typical metal man, and her best friend.

Jamie smiled, knowing exactly what he wanted. "Sure," she said, before he had a chance to ask.

Monty chuckled. "Got me all figured out already, eh twit?"

She set her clipboard down and gave him her full attention. "If we didn't do this routine every day, then I might wonder why you're walking toward me after lunch ended."

He unrolled his pack of smokes from the shoulder of his T-shirt and joined her on the picnic table. "The boss wants moose meat for our new guests tonight."

Jamie eyeballed him. "Since when do we keep wild game off-season?"

"We don't."

She stared at him in confused silence as Monty lit his cigarette, closed his eyes, and took a deep drag. After a long moment of suspense he glanced back at her with a sly grin. "But we have lots of beef."

"Ah." Jamie laughed as she scammed one of his cigarettes. "And you expect to pull this off without suspicion?"

He shrugged and handed over his lighter. "I'll just add some crazy seasoning. The city folk won't know the difference. Besides, Valerie is to blame if I get caught. She told them they were getting a wild northern meal."

Jamie shook her head. "You're an ass, you know that? Why not just cook up some pickerel for your *wild northern meal*?"

The door to the lodge whipped open and the person in question stepped out, shielding her eyes from the glaring sun. "There you are," the boss said, her face flushed, her voice rising with hysteria. Valerie stared past Jamie. Even though Monty tried his best to hide behind her, his huge frame allowed no such thing. "Monty! Mrs. Westwood would like another salad."

Jamie pursed her lips to halt a burst of laughter. One might've thought the kitchen was on fire by Valerie's horrified expression—over a salad.

"Ugh." Monty stood and snubbed out his half smoke on the edge of the picnic table. "I don't know why she can't do it herself. Obviously she has no idea how frustrating it is cooking all summer for these people while she mingles and smiles." He leaned closer to add, "But rumor has it she's losing money, you know. I've noticed she's been drinking more than usual lately. I think she's getting ready to sell."

Jamie's stomach flipped and she sucked in a sharp breath. Valerie promised to give her a loan to catch up on some hefty bills as long as Jamie promised to work off that debt. Rent was past due and her landlord had already threatened to evict her if she didn't catch up when she returned at the end of the season. That wasn't her only worry. She stared down at the lawn as another fear gripped her. The past had a terrible way of racing up to people and slapping them in the face. When you owe money to a dangerous person, well, either you catch up fast or you get broken. This had to be the worst year of her life, but she wouldn't admit the truth to Monty. He'd call her more than a twit if he knew what shady deal she'd messed up back at home because of a dark past she wanted to forget.

She forced a tight smile. "I'm sure it's just a rumor. You know Jobe is always causing shit."

Monty nodded. "True. Want to switch jobs? I bet you could do a decent job whipping up a salad."

Brushing off her personal worries, Jamie glanced up at him and arched a brow. "And I bet you could do a decent job wiping out a toilet."

He grimaced as he rolled his smokes back up into his T-shirt. "Never mind. That's a woman's job."

Monty retreated to the back door leading into the kitchen, but not quickly enough for her to shout back, "Kiss my womanly ass!" She continued staring as the screen door smacked behind him. Since day one working at Sharp Ridge Lodge five years ago, they hit it off as immediate friends, only to find out they lived right around the corner from each other in the city. Even though Monty was a good man with a big heart, not once did she ever think to strike up a relationship with him. Her love and appreciation for the man never went beyond friendship. Besides, the thought of kissing a man whose mustache curled over his lips made her cringe.

After a good stretch, Jamie hopped off the picnic table, grabbed the clipboard, and headed toward the laundry building to put her cleaning basket together and gather up the linens she needed.

A groundhog scurried across the lawn and disappeared underneath one of the guest quarters. Those little buggers were everywhere around here, but they caused no trouble to the staff or the guests. The skunks were another matter altogether. Groundskeeper Jobe was about to blow his wig if he had to catch another one of them black and white devils. Jamie loved to accompany him as he set his live trap boxes then brought the furry beasts out to an island to inhabit. The very island the yearly canoeists liked to camp on.

Bringing the skunks to the island was a funny little joke between the staff at Sharp Ridge Lodge. While they didn't want to kill the skunks, they didn't want them stinking up the lodge grounds either. Since the canoeists tended to get in the way of the fishermen, Jobe came up with the idea to let the skunks and the canoeists have their very own island. Every once in a while a scream could be heard echoing over the lake in the direction of Skunk Island.

Over the next two hours Jamie set up the cabins for the elderly guests and the honeymoon couple. The last cabin to prepare was for the mystery man with no leaving date. After the bathroom sparkled and the floors gleamed, she set out making the bed with hunter green cotton sheets and a floral comforter set in the same deep green. Even the window curtains had the same floral pattern—green being the color of all linen on site with pops of hot pink and yellow. Even though Jamie didn't care for any type of floral pattern, she had to admit it gave the cabins a cozy, almost Hawaiian vibe.

She had just finished her final walk-through to make sure she hadn't missed anything when the distinct rumble of the float plane soared over the lodge. Jamie grabbed her basket, closed the cabin door, and headed back to the laundry building to complete her washing.

Once her chores were completed for the day, she headed up the path that curved around a thicket of pine, poplar, and mountain ash, toward her cabin overlooking the grounds. She changed into her bathing suit, grabbed a towel, and headed down to the swimming hole next to the cliffs that lined the west side of the property. Sometimes she and Monty would jump or dive off those twenty-foot cliffs. Today, she decided on a leisure swim just beneath them.

The new arrivals would be in the dining lounge right now enjoying their wild northern meal, then mingle with other guests and staff before retiring to their cabins for the night. Tomorrow the fun of fishing expeditions, hiking trails, or games would begin. Valerie always had something fun planned for the guests. They could enjoy outings as a group if they chose, or just do whatever they desired on their own. They could even take a guide out with them if they weren't comfortable navigating the twenty-thousand acre lake on their own.

She dove into the murky water, so dark she couldn't see a foot past her face, and frog-swam beneath the surface as far as her lungs would take her. When she crested the top, she released a content, invigorated sigh from the cool water on such a hot day. She repeated this move several times, back and forth from shore—a ritual she performed as much as she could handle.

The distant hum of a boat motor echoed across the bay. A couple of ravens squawked at each other nearby. A tiny avalanche of pebbles skidded down the steep slope beside the cliffs. Jamie swung her body around in the water and glanced up at the cliff, her gaze halting on a man standing there watching her.

He withdrew one hand from the pocket of his jogging pants and waved. "Hey there. Sorry if I scared you. I came across a trail and found this spot."

Something in his mouth glinted in the sunlight. "It's okay. You must be one of the new guests. I'm Jamie, your housekeeper."

"Nice to meet you, Jamie. I'm Jack."

The mysterious Jack Daniels. "Nice to meet you, Jack. What brings you to our little paradise in the woods?" Jamie's arms were beginning to tire from treading water for too long, but she had no plans to drag herself out and climb up that hill just to shake his hand. She could introduce herself properly later on in the lounge. Swimming after work was her private time.

His soft chuckle made goose bumps slip down her arms. "I thought everyone came to places like this for peace and quiet?"

"Depends if you're fishing or hunting I suppose, although small game season doesn't start for another couple of weeks." From where she treaded water, he looked like he could be the bushman type. He stood strong and confident; wide shoulders tapered to a lean waist. A thick black beard concealed most of his face, and he wore a baseball cap. But from this distance, she couldn't make out any fine details about his features.

"I'll probably do some fishing, but no hunting for me anyway."

Jamie laughed and stretched her arms out, moving in a fluid motion a short distance from where she had treaded water. It was getting harder and harder to keep her chin above the water. "Not the hunting type, *Jack*?" She wanted to end the conversation and get back to shore.

"I don't believe in killing animals."

"Good to know. It's not hunting season anyway." Despite her exhaustion, Jamie smiled when he laughed. "Well, maybe I'll see you later. You're more than welcome to join us all in the lounge this evening. It's kind of a ritual around here." She started swimming toward the low end of the shore while she still had enough strength not to drown in front of him.

"Sure," he called out as she disappeared around the cliff face.

As soon as she reached the first flat boulder just beneath the surface of the water, she climbed on top and let out an exhausted groan. Every muscle in her arms screamed that she'd pushed herself too far, but she loved the water. In her eyes, drowning would probably be the best way to go.

Once she regained her breath and her strength, she made it to shore and wrapped the towel around her body. Something made her look over her shoulder toward the area of the cliffs at the dense brush hiding the walking path behind. She didn't see him there, but she wondered if the stranger had watched her swim back, or if he stood there watching her now.

* * * *

Later that night a strong autumn breeze swished through the trees as twilight fell over Sharp Ridge Lodge. Jamie headed down the path from her cabin surrounded by darkness, yet she knew by heart exactly where to step, having walked these grounds many times over her five years working here. She knew everything by heart. Twenty-eight steps down the path until she reached the flat expanse of the lawn. Eight steps to the right she would reach the first of three woodsheds, then the guest cabins, and then the lodge just beyond. Although Valerie insisted that staff carry a flashlight at night, Jamie had no need for it. The mystery of the woods with the frogs croaking all around the path was just one intriguing part of working and living here.

The property of the camp itself would be equivalent to three football fields, and beyond the grounds stretched for hundreds of miles in every direction. This site could only be accessed by float plane, helicopter, or portaging from the nearest village.

Shady Grace

Communication with the outside world consisted of a CB radio used to call in the weather report and to call the base post in town. Other than that, the only connection the staff had with family was by written letter. Every day a plane arrived either with guests or supplies, and sometimes both. It came as no surprise to Jamie at all if the plane was full of passengers and gear with a boat tied to each float. If she had a dollar for every time a plane barely crested the treetops, then maybe she wouldn't be in debt.

A familiar sound carried along the wind. Jamie smiled as Valerie's loud cackle blew every other sound out of the water. She must be regaling the guests with stories of past adventures to strumming every banjo tune she knew. Jamie didn't mind her boss's silly ways, as long as she didn't force her to dance with some horny old man like Jobe. Then again, maybe she'd actually get laid if she did.

The cool air swished up her naked legs. She stopped on the path and looked back through the black void, wondering if she should change from shorts and tank top into something warmer. A storm must be brewing as it often did this time of year.

I'll be warm inside the lodge anyway. She continued along the path. One of the staff would have a fire going on a chilly night like this.

As Jamie opened the main door, a haze of cigarette and cigar smoke filled the room. Most of the twelve guests on site were gathered around the massive stone fireplace, listening to Valerie repeat one of her famous stories.

"...and he almost hooked his nose when the fish spit out the Daredevil, that poor man. I think he learned pretty quickly not to stand up in the boat and yank too hard on his rod!"

The crowd erupted with laughter. Valerie's cheeks were flushed with excitement and too much to drink. She waved her arms around, creating more hype for the story; booze swished over the rim of her glass, spattering on the floor beside her.

Jamie chuckled as she ambled up beside Monty, amazed to see him wearing a checkered button-down shirt and slacks instead of the usual skull-and-bones gear. Valerie must've dressed him tonight. She quirked an amused brow and leaned against a log post behind the guests. "How many has she had?"

"About half a dozen, I guess."

"No wonder she's so loud. That woman can't handle her booze."

Monty chuckled and glanced out over the crowd. "Yeah, but they love her."

He was right. Everyone watched her in rapt fascination as she continued on with another story about a group of men who were lost on the lake during a storm. Everyone listened intently to every word. Except for one man. His attention was fixed on Jamie.

Jamie swallowed as her gaze met his and held. She'd always thought the saying "there was something about him that I couldn't resist" was utterly pathetic, and yet, that was exactly how she felt right now as they stared at each other. It seemed like this Jack Daniels guy had a temporary spell over her. His dark eyes, glowing amber in the firelight, held her in their grip. A slow, sexy grin curved his full lips. An exciting thrill rushed through her at the sudden and unexpected urge to step outside into the darkness and let him kiss her under the stars.

Wow. She released a shuddering breath as her stomach cinched just from looking at him.

"Want a drink?"

"Hmm?"

Monty smacked her shoulder, ripping her away from her heated thoughts. She blinked up at him. "What?"

"I asked if you wanted a drink. But by the look on your face, maybe you've had a few already."

Her cheeks burned as she elbowed him in the ribs. "Shut up." She gathered her wits and walked away from him, making her way around the small counter they used for an open bar, made of hand-peeled logs from the property. Oddly enough, she chose Jack and Coke for her evening beverage. What she really needed was that wild encounter outside.

She drank the whole thing down in under a minute, ignoring the quizzical glance from Monty. As she poured a second, an intoxicating scent of vanilla and spice assaulted her senses.

"So we meet again."

That voice did something to every tiny hair on her body. It rung smooth and deep like the narrator of a nature documentary—the kind with mating animals. Her heart thudded hard. When she looked up, Jamie knew it would be the mystery stud with a fake-sounding name. It had to be fake, or maybe she just watched too many suspense movies lately, having no cable out here.

"You're not wet any more," he murmured.

Is he talking dirty to me, or is he just being friendly? That sexy grin wreaked havoc on her nerves. She didn't know how to respond. She'd had her flings in the past, but none of those men talked to her as if she should be petted and licked and plucked for hours. Or maybe she was too drunk or stoned back then to remember a man making her feel so flushed.

Now she saw him up close, and he had the kind of features that made women automatically feel good. His skin was light brown, his lips perfectly generous, framed by a thick and curly black beard. The tight black curls of his short hair spoke subtly of his mixed heritage as well. He had a sexy, hard-bodied look that could easily grace the cover of a sports magazine. His biceps practically ripped out of the sleeves of his blood-red T-shirt— the color accentuating his complexion as if a fashion guru had picked the shirt for that purpose.

Jamie sucked in a sharp breath. Her instant attraction could be sealed in an envelope. She blushed as his bold gaze swept over her. He studied her so intently it made a hot ache bloom between her legs. Embarrassed, she averted her gaze and looked back down at her drink as the corner of her mouth twitched. Maybe she should've made a double.

But she couldn't help a flirty response of her own. As Jamie stirred her drink, she forced herself to look back up and reply, "Such a shame I'm not wet anymore."

Her nerves skipped to life as he chuckled and eased against the counter on one elbow, his back facing the rest of the crowd. Apparently he didn't care to be a part of the festivities. "Being wet is much more exciting than being dry."

"It is." *That's it? You can't think of something better than that?* She cleared her throat and tried to come up with something sexy to say, something to really grab him by the nuts, but her brain couldn't think beyond gripping his collar and yanking him over the bar for a kiss. She seriously wanted to know how those lips would feel against hers. "Do you like to swim, Mr. Daniels?"

His hot gaze traveled down to her breasts, then back up. "Sometimes, but I prefer a steamy, *naked* sauna."

Jesus Christ. Right to the point. "Well, you can use the sauna any time you'd like, naked or dressed." She shrugged off her growing discomfort. "Whatever you'd like."

"*Whatever* I'd like?"

Her wide gaze met his and held. Her panties were soaked. Her nipples were tight, and by the heat of his gaze as it lowered to her chest, she knew they must be noticeable. Jamie wanted nothing more than to have screaming, hot sex in the sauna with this man right now, but she couldn't. They had rules here, and staff could not have flings with customers. Such a shame. She had a feeling he'd fuck her silly.

Jack seemed to catch on to her sudden withdraw, and gave a brief, almost disappointed nod. "So what should I do to pass the time? I'm getting a little bored of the old people in the room."

She held her snort of laughter in check. "Not everyone is old."

He looked over her body again, slowly, as if somebody had punched up the heat to a blistering degree. "How old are you? If you don't mind me asking."

"Thirty-one next month."

His grin widened and she saw what that golden gleam was from earlier. The last time she'd seen a gold tooth was on a music video. But it suited Mr. Daniels to a T, in a sensual, reckless, *I make my own rules*, kind of way.

"You're in your prime, then. That's good," he murmured.

Jamie's eyes widened again. Apparently she couldn't hide her shocked reaction to everything that came out of his mouth. He sure had a bold way with words. By rights the powder on her cheeks should melt they burned so hard. "How old are you? If you don't mind me asking."

"Thirty-nine last month."

A warm sensation from the first drink—or maybe from the man in front of her—settled right between her legs. "I guess you're in your prime, too," she answered with as much sass as she could muster, and before she made a complete fool of herself, Jamie grabbed her glass and stepped around the bar. "Have a good evening, Mr. Daniels." She left him standing there watching her, and went straight to Monty to pepper him with boring chat for the rest of the evening.

Breathe. Focus. Breathe. Stop creaming in your panties.

No man had ever been that brash with her before, and she'd never responded so easily like that either. She felt excited and nervous and more excited. Under the cover of her lashes, she watched as the sexy stranger poured himself a drink and returned to his seat. She stared, transfixed and soaking wet as her gaze swept over his backside. God, his body was built like Granite Island which was only a short boat ride away.

She looked away and chided herself. Since when did she react like a love swept dimwit to a man? Maybe it was the seven months spent in the grip of her vibrator that turned her into a desperate female. She hadn't had a real man since Pete, and he was over a year ago.

"I'm going outside for a smoke. Want to come with me?"

Monty shook his head and laughed. "I just had one. I couldn't bear to handle the corny steam at the bar a moment ago." He plopped his arm across her shoulders, the weight of it pushing her down. "That's exactly what you need though."

Mortified by his obvious meaning, Jamie lifted the glass and took a sip before answering. "What are you talking about?"

He leaned down and whispered in a teasing tone, "I'm saying you should bang that guy. Hell, if I swung that way, I would. He's pretty hot."

Jamie was just taking another drink and choked on it. "You're completely insane. Valerie would fire me, and you know it. I don't even know him"— she looked around to make sure nobody heard their conversation—"and I've never fucked a stranger before."

Monty pulled back and let out a loud bark of laughter. Valerie stopped talking, all heads turned toward them, and Jamie wanted to die. She stood there beside him, eyes wide, having no clue what to say.

Good thing Monty quickly corrected his sudden outburst and added, "Valerie always tells the best stories, doesn't she?"

Even though Jamie and Monty had no idea what Valerie had been saying at the time, apparently the guests agreed with him. They all applauded the host and she basked in their attention.

Monty leaned down and whispered, "Remember that older woman last summer who had eyes for me?" Jamie nodded, curious yet unsure if she wanted to hear what crazy story he intended to brag about. "Let's just say the pole struck bottom every single night she was here."

Jamie blinked and stared up at him, knowing what he meant but not wanting to hear any more. He added, "What Val doesn't know doesn't hurt her, or anyone else. People fuck at work all the time."

Monty straightened and stared out over the crowd, a knowing smile on his face. Jamie took the opportunity to escape for a smoke and get some much-needed fresh air. Maybe she should continue her little erotic sparring with Jack. It would definitely get her mind off of the bad things swirling in her head like a fatal disease. *Just a few minutes to forget all that bad shit, please!*

She discreetly moved back into the dim lamplight by the lodge entrance and stepped outside, gently closing the big wooden door behind her. The wind had picked up more since she left her cabin, but that didn't stop her from heading down to the dock and appreciating the beauty of the darkness around her. A sliver of a moon reflected dancing crystals over the water. Waves lapped softly against the dock and the shoreline.

This was therapy right here. Sharp Ridge Lodge had a serenity yet thrill about it that she didn't want to leave. Soon she would have no choice, just like the others. Everybody was bound to return to regular life.

The wind shifted and a familiar scent swept past her. She knew it was him from that spicy vanilla cologne. Knew it like the surety of the murky water beneath the dock.

She turned around. "Tired of the old people again, Jack?"

"Something like that."

He was less than two feet away. She barely made out his features, and that was just fine for her. Nothing compared to the thrill and the mystery of the night.

She turned away from him and stared back out over the water. Every nerve jumped to life by his proximity. He was a stranger, and yet she couldn't help her body's response to his nearness. Until now she'd never believed in pure lust at first sight.

"Nothing compares to this, you know," she said aloud.

He stepped closer, and she knew he was staring at her profile instead of the water. "Nope."

Jamie swallowed. This was becoming hot and heavy right fast. She didn't know this guy any more than her mailman in the city. Maybe he was just a player who'd bang any girl he met. Maybe she shouldn't worry so much and just have fun, as long as she played safe. She didn't really know what to do, or what to say to him. Sticking with idle chat seemed like the safest choice. "Why the open leaving date?"

A long moment passed before he answered. "It's hard for me to plan time off with my schedule. I could leave next month, next week…who knows?"

Despite the humor in his tone, she suspected he told the truth, and that the rest of it wasn't so simple. "Well, I'm sure you'll enjoy it here, for however long that will be."

"I'm sure I will."

The sound of water lapping against the dock seemed to stretch on for long, awkward minutes. "So, how did you find out about Sharp Ridge?"

"I found a pamphlet for this place in a jacket pocket."

She chuckled. "That sounds kind of strange, Jack. Did it fall out of some guy's coat or something?"

He cleared his throat. "Something like that."

Jamie jerked when he stepped closer and his shoulder brushed against hers. He was too close. Too much too soon. Her body screamed to touch him yet her mind shouted to behave at her place of work. "Well, I should head home. I have an early start. Have a good—"

"Do I scare you, Jamie?" He turned to her, his face expressionless in the dark. "I'm not a nutjob or anything. Just a man who happens to like what he sees."

She swallowed. "I'm not afraid of you. Just…nervous." How could she tell him she felt an immediate and thrilling attraction without sounding pathetic? She certainly wouldn't tell him how long it had been since the last time she had sex. Somehow she knew a night under the sheets with him would be hot and sweaty and unforgettable.

"Being nervous is a good thing. It means you have passion for life."

She didn't know how to answer that other than a pitiful, "Maybe."

When he leaned closer, she knew what he wanted. For the life of her she wouldn't deny it, no matter how crazy it seemed. In a hot second his lips brushed over hers as his thumb skimmed softly under the curve of her jaw. Like the striking of a match, a flame flickered through her like fire through dry brush. It was as if they were meant to meet in this spot, on this dock, on this windy night.

Jamie felt weightless and heavy at the same time as he explored her, tasted her; made her thighs tremble and her hands shake at her sides. Wanting him closer, Jamie reached up and feathered her fingers through his tight curls. Her body formed against his as his hand snaked around her waist. He felt wonderful. His scent intoxicated her. The way he boldly held her made her feel weak and needy like the women in those corny romance novels.

Minutes ticked by as they moaned and ground against each other in the darkness. It was as if she had no control over herself, no thought of consequence as his hands curved over her bum, squeezing and gripping, pressing her harder against his erection.

They panted in unison. Their tongues sucked and swirled and mated.

"*Jamie?*"

Her eyes opened wide at the sound of Valerie's voice calling out in the night. She stilled, pulled away from Jack, and glanced at the lodge. The boss woman hung out the door, probably needing her assistance for something, her body silhouetted by the interior lights behind her. Thank God Valerie couldn't see them standing there in the dark.

The hard swell of Jack's cock pressed hard and hot against her, a rampant reminder of what exactly transpired. She would've fucked him right there. Right on the dock without any protection, she was that desperate and horny. He hadn't even spent a single night here yet and already the housekeeper would've rode him until the dock broke away from shore.

Embarrassed and beyond ashamed, Jamie pushed away and backed up. "I'm so sorry. I...." She clamped her lips shut, spun around, and ran up the dock steps to the second tier without looking back. How could she do that to herself? Did she have no control at all over her body? He must think her a total slut.

By the time she reached the lawn in front of the lodge, Valerie had already disappeared back inside. Hopefully she had forgotten about Jamie, or simply lost interest in finding her. Either way, Jamie was relieved that Valerie hadn't seen what happened. Jamie glanced over her shoulder to see if Jack had followed, but only darkness surrounded her. Shaking hard and panting for air, she quickly composed herself and walked in, hoping to God she didn't give away what she had almost done. Valerie would be furious.

"There you are. Outside smoking again?" Valerie asked, smiling like a Cheshire cat. She swayed on her feet, and Jamie realized she'd never seen her boss that drunk before. Maybe Monty had been right about her losing money, and that was a terrifying thought. A sudden chill that had nothing to do with the weather outside made her tremble. *What if Jones sends somebody after me?*

"Are you cold?" Monty asked, his voice laced with humor.

Jamie cleared her throat and forced a straight face. *I wish my only problem was being cold.* "Yeah. Sorry I took so long. I had my feet in the water."

"Oh, that's nice." Valerie's gaze seemed to be barely focused on Jamie's shoulder.

Monty, standing behind Valerie yet towering over her, arched a high brow. "Did you fall onto the second tier of the dock? You look a little flushed and rumpled."

Jamie avoided his probing stare, especially the teasing tone of his annoying voice, and focused on Valerie instead. "I'm fine, really."

"But where's Mr. Daniels? I saw him leave right after you," Monty added and waggled his eyebrows.

Jamie glared at him, then turned her attention back to Valerie again. "I saw someone walking toward the guest quarters. I'm sure it was him."

"Oh, he must be exhausted. That retail business will bring a man to an early grave," Valerie slurred, completely clueless to the almost sex with a stranger that just happened on her dock.

"Yes. I'm sure you're right." Jamie patted Valerie's shoulder. The poor woman was going to have a wicked hangover come morning. "Well, I'm calling it a night. See you bright and early." Jamie glared at the grinning Monty and retreated back outside. When she returned to her cabin, she pulled out her vibrator from the nightstand and took him to bed. Within three minutes she shuddered hard on his buzzing shaft, her whole body tingling, vividly remembering the sensation of Jack's stiff cock against her.

It was big.

As she drifted into a restless sleep, Jamie had a feeling that tonight wouldn't be her last encounter with the mysterious Jack Daniels.

"Tomorrow," she whispered in the darkness. "Tomorrow, I won't be so afraid of you."

Chapter 3

A branch gently scraped against the window pane in Sam's cabin early the next morning. He stood at the window looking out over the grey dawn sky and the placid water of Sharp Ridge Lake. A low mist hung over the shoreline across the bay. A Great Blue Heron stood in the shallows near a cluster of cattails. The promise of a dreary day loomed ahead, but he didn't mind. What he really wanted was to get that housekeeper over here to double check his bed linen. A really close look with her face down—ass up.

Sam released a disgruntled breath and shook his head. Unbelievable how quickly he'd gone from having a simple conversation with the beautiful woman, to nearly plowing her right on that dock last night. He felt a strange attraction to her—something he'd never felt before with a woman. He liked that she enjoyed nature and lived out here during the summer months. It made him envious. Sam rarely had the chance to enjoy life while he took away someone else's. Maybe that's exactly what he deserved.

A group of fishermen crossed the lawn not too far from his cabin. They carried their gear to the boats lined up along the small docks, all of them smiling and eager to get their hooks in the water. Sam watched as the group set their tackle, rods, and minnow buckets into two boats. The outboard motors were yanked alive, and the hum of the engines brought life to the silence as they pulled away from shore.

Sam was just about to leave his cabin and fetch a cup of coffee from the main lodge when his satellite phone shrieked through the cabin.

Ugh. He let the curtain fall back and grabbed the phone from the side pocket of his suitcase. He knew it wouldn't stop ringing if he didn't answer. This was his emergency line only and he didn't go anywhere without it.

He barked into the receiver, "What the hell is so important that you call me on my vacation? Did somebody actually die?"

"A-are you a-lone?"

Sam barely made out the scratchy voice over the static on the phone. "You'll have to speak up. I'm in the middle of nowhere."

"Are you alone?"

"Yeah, why?"

"I need you to come home. I'll explain later." He knew immediately it was Terry and it had to be important. Sam had stressed to Terry not to call while he was on vacation unless somebody died. As much as he wanted to ignore the request and continue with his time away, if something dreadful happened, then he'd feel responsible for not taking immediate action.

The urge to growl made him grit his teeth. So much for a well-deserved vacation far from anybody he knew. After hearing all the stories from Terry and Gabe about life in the woods with their women, he had become envious. Finding this place in the deep north of Ontario had been a blessing, although very short-lived. Plans never worked out for a man like him. Work never ended.

"I'll be on the first flight out."

He ended the call and ambled up to the window, drew the curtains open again. He could get used to this stunning view, even with the grey sky and lurking fog. After nearly twenty years of being the gunman behind the McCoy Empire, he just wanted peace and quiet like the rest of them.

Gabe and Terry had their futures mapped out, while Sam felt like a wanderer destined to a life all alone. His brothers were busy with their women and Sam was afraid of that kind of commitment. He couldn't promise to survive the night, let alone make it to dinner on time. What woman would want that kind of life? On top of that, he enjoyed the thrill of the chase, the terrifying excitement of knowing that a bullet could end it all at any second. Nothing could be more hair-raising than living on impulse.

Gabe tied the knot with Mima last fall and Terry and Mary had their second child already. Sam had nothing but his suitcase, a cache of prized weapons, and good ol' Auntie Rose.

But he'd like something soft. Something that meant something. Someone to turn to on those nights when he truly felt alone. He wasn't afraid to admit that life scared him. Many a night he'd wake up stunned, as if he expected to be smothered in his sleep by a rival hitman as he had done once before on assignment. Or he'd wake up in a pool of sweat, often from the same dream of driving in his car, only to have the brakes fail from being cut, and plummeting into a deep gorge to his death. He probably deserved that fate, too, especially after hearing on the news that the man in the gorge had survived down there for three days before he died from his injuries. That recurring nightmare was a punishment Sam had accepted long ago.

This wasn't a job for everyone. Sometimes it wasn't a job for him, although most of the time he enjoyed flying to each corner of the earth and being pampered at luxurious hotels and chauffeured around like a king. Still, sometimes he imagined what it would be like to sit back in a cozy living room in front of a fireplace with a glass of wine, or even a cup of tea, or maybe have a cold beer with friends in the backyard—as long as nobody got shot.

He stared down at his suitcase and shook his head. He hadn't even unzipped it yet. Hadn't even put his toothbrush onto the bathroom vanity. That thought alone made him feel really tired. Sometimes it felt as if his life meant nothing more than taking on another job, and never getting the chance to enjoy the meaning of life. Did the boys not realize how unhappy he'd become? How much he felt like a chess piece, waiting for somebody to move him? Despite the bitter taste in his mouth that they hadn't noticed his change in demeanor, while they enjoyed their lives and women, Sam wouldn't let the depression get to him. They deserved their slice of happiness. Maybe he didn't.

Sam often wondered what life would have been like if he didn't meet Colton that day. He could've gotten to know his parents better. Maybe they stayed away because he chose this precarious path of life at such a young age. Sometimes he wondered if they had tried to be better parents, only to discover that he had no intention of being a regular, blue-collar son. But it was the path he chose, and whether or not he became tired of the routine, this was all that he knew. He had no other skills to fall back upon. Well, unless he became a hunting guide. That sudden thought made him think a little harder about a life in the open bush with a rifle in his arms—rather than concealing a handgun in a busy train station.

He violently shut the curtains, cursing aloud, and went back to bed, even if only for a few more minutes. As he lounged back against the pillows with the bedside lamp still on, he thought of all the places where he'd traveled, all the faces that came and went, and all the good things in life that he never had a chance to enjoy.

Maybe he could have a woman right now. A couple of kids. A life. But what kind of woman wanted a man who lived through the eye of a scope? He'd have to trust her completely, or lie to her indefinitely. To Sam, that was no way to live. He was better off being alone, because he had nothing special to offer anyone. Nothing but a life of constant worry.

He stared up at the wood paneling on the ceiling, forcing his thoughts away from his constant turmoil. He liked the décor of this place. It was rustic but pleasant, sort of homey in an eighties Miami hotel kind of way.

A movement caught his eye. He stared, transfixed, as a huge spider crawled out of a crack in the boards. The eight-legged creature stopped for a moment, probably eyeing its prey, before it scurried across the length of the ceiling and disappeared. He felt like that spider, destined to hunt until it spun its last web and killed its next mate.

Five minutes later and more frustrated than ever, Sam shoved off the bed and grabbed his belongings. He walked into the lodge with his suitcase in hand to find the lodge owner sitting at a table with her head in her hands. Either she had a wicked hangover or something else weighed on her brain.

He cleared his throat and she whipped her head up, blinking rapidly.

"Good morning," Sam said, and pulled a chair out across from her.

He guessed by her immediate smile that it had been well practiced over the years. "Good morning, Mr. Daniels. What brings you in here so early? I'm afraid the coffee isn't"—her gaze landed on the suitcase—"ready yet." She appeared startled as her red-eyed gaze darted from the suitcase back to him. "Is there a problem with your cabin?"

"No, the cabin was great." He offered an apologetic smile. "Duty calls, I'm afraid. Will there be a plane coming in this morning?"

"You're lucky. We have two flights coming in today. The first plane should be arriving any minute, and the second will be around noon." She stared at him sharply. "How were you able to get phone service?"

"I carry a satellite phone. It works pretty much everywhere."

"Ah. The retail business must be lucrative."

He chuckled. If that's what she wanted to believe, so be it. "Well, as long as it isn't any trouble, I'll take the first flight out."

Valerie smiled sadly and offered her hand for a shake. "Of course not. Well, we hope you return soon for a proper visit, Mr. Daniels. I'll be sure to refund your money right away."

He lifted his hand in refusal. "That isn't necessary."

"But—"

"I insist you keep it. I'm sure it costs quite a lot to charter planes around here. I happen to know a little about that, and since I'm leaving prematurely, it's only fair that you keep the money."

Valerie nodded and made no further comment. He sensed she was uncomfortable over the discussion of money.

The main door opened and two burly-looking men stepped inside with their baggage and fishing gear. Sam remembered them from last night as they hooted and hollered with the rest of them. They looked pale-faced and red-eyed this morning, almost as bad as the host.

Valerie's instant grin was in hard play this morning as she pushed her chair back and stood to greet the men. "Mr. Daniels will be joining you on the flight out this morning, guys."

Valerie turned to Sam. "The Bailey brothers have been coming here for over ten years," she said proudly. "Same time every year, and we're happy to have them." Their host turned away to set out coffee cups and the fixings. "Coffee is ready. You three gentlemen come get a cup now before the plane gets here."

As Sam and the two brothers sipped on the strong brew, he wondered when the housekeeper started her duties for the day. He imagined she must be embarrassed by their encounter last night. He, on the other hand, was blown away by the instant attraction. But that thought didn't last long as the engine of the plane rumbled over the lodge. Sam stood and wandered to a nearby picture window, casually sipping the strong brew, and watched its descent. Any time he had the pleasure to watch a plane in action he always thought of Gabe. That man could fly anything anywhere. He wondered briefly if the boys would be interested in this sort of business. Now that Terry was out of the illegal loop, enjoying life with Mary and the kids, and Gabe living an adventurous life in the mountains with Mima, Sam wondered if they'd be interested in partnering up on a legitimate business. Something they could all operate together. Or even for all of them to use as a private vacation spot. There must be other lodges around for a potential sale. Maybe he should set up a meeting with the boys and hear their thoughts on the idea. Sam couldn't imagine their partnership being over just because the empire had ended. They were still his brothers. His fucked-up little family meant everything to him.

The float plane, a twin Otter, swooped in a great circle over the trees, and made a smooth landing in the bay. As it taxied toward the dock, one of the dock hands waited with rope in hand for the plane to reach him.

Sam turned around and smiled at Valerie. "It was a pleasure while it lasted. Maybe I'll see you next season."

That winning smile seemed to fade as she nodded her head. Sam wondered if running a lodge was as wonderful as it was cracked up to be. But he thought no more of it as he had more important things to worry about. If Terry needed him home right now, then some bad shit was about to go down—if it hadn't already.

He grabbed his suitcase and headed down to the dock. As the pilot maneuvered the great beast into the air and swept around to fly over the lodge, Sam wondered what was so important to Terry that Sam had to cut his vacation short before it had a chance to start.

* * * *

"I don't understand. I thought everything was okay." Jamie fought the urge to bawl like a child as Valerie's bad news hit home. Now she understood why the boss lady had been drinking so much lately.

"I've been losing money three years in a row. I can't afford to keep this place going after the remaining guests leave."

Jamie ripped a few tissues out of the box on Valerie's desk and dried her tears. "What exactly are you saying? Are you firing me?"

Valerie lowered her chin and stared down at her desk for a long while. Jamie thought that she too was trying to put on a brave face. "No, I'd never fire you, sweetheart." When she looked back up, Jamie recognized the honesty in her eyes. "I just can't afford to give you that loan, and as of today I have to lay you off. Right now I need a guide and a dockhand more than anything. I'll have to clean the cabins and do all the cooking myself." Her sharp stare cut Jamie right to the core. "I'm so sorry, honey. I thought I could pull through till the end of the season, but I was horribly wrong. I should've shut 'er down last year."

Jamie's chin quivered. A knot the size of a golf ball lodged in her throat. *This can't be happening. Not now.* "Does Monty know about this, too?" When Valerie nodded, she almost broke down in hysterical sobbing. So they both were up shit creek without a canoe. "What am I supposed to do? I'm so far in debt I'll be ruined."

"I'm sorry, Jamie, I really am. I've tried everything. I've even drained all of my savings. I just can't do this any more. I have enough funds to pay you and Monty up until today. Any money owing from the remaining guests will cover my final operating costs. I'll be forced to sell as quickly as I can or go bankrupt and abandon this place."

"What about investors?" Jamie jumped up from her seat and paced Valerie's office. She had ideas. They could try something—anything to keep the lodge in operation. She couldn't imagine her favorite place in the world being abandoned.

"I've tried, believe me, I've tried everything." Valerie stood from the desk and approached Jamie, her eyes glistening with tears. "You've been a wonderful asset to this lodge, my dear. If I manage to sell, everyone here will be recommended to come back. I promise."

Jamie had no more words to say. Her mind was running a mile a minute wondering what she would do when she returned home. She wouldn't have enough hours from the season to collect unemployment insurance by going home a month early. How was she supposed to survive? She needed that loan more than anything just to be able to keep her tiny apartment in the city, and having been fostered, she had no living relatives to seek shelter. No bank would give her a loan from a seasonal job either, and the time it would take to find a job in the city and collect a paycheck, it would be too late.

She suspected Valerie was struggling, but this was too much to take. "Well, I guess there isn't much else to say. I'm really sorry this is happening to you, but I don't know what to do now. Maybe I could speak to that Jack Daniels guy and beg him for a job in whatever retail business he's in." It was just a joke, but at this point she had nothing else to lose. Didn't Valerie say he was a man of business?

Valerie shook her head. "I'm afraid he left yesterday."

Jamie spun around and blinked hard. "What? But he just got here."

"Apparently he had a satellite phone and got a call to return to work. He flew out yesterday morning. I was actually sad to see him go. He looked like a man with money."

No wonder she hadn't seen him since that night. Jamie's heart sank. *Oh God.* He probably escaped after she threw herself at him like a hard-up hooker. Now she felt truly, utterly hopeless and pathetic, downright disgusted by her behavior that night. He must have been eager to get away. The call from work was probably a lie. *Nobody travels to a lodge in the middle of nowhere with a fucking satellite phone.*

She had nobody to ask for help, and with Monty's layoff as well, he would be tight for money, too. Jamie had already taxed out her propositions for housekeeping in the city, and she didn't have time to find another job when she owed so much money already.

She couldn't say for sure what had pulled her into the world of selling dope. Maybe it seemed like the cool thing to do at the time. Her memories were blurry at best, and that was her own fault. The smart kids in high school, who were going somewhere with their lives, were in a whole other world than Jamie ever could be in. Perhaps following the rough crowd back then seemed easier, considering her family life had been precarious at best. But selling a few joints, or a few bags of blow was one thing—doing your own shit was another.

That's how she got in a bad way. She became dependent on cocaine, and in the end, right before she smartened up, she'd borrowed a large amount, only to get ripped off by a thug. Now she was caught in a dangerous game, owing money to somebody who could seriously hurt her.

With more tears in her eyes and an emptiness in her heart, Jamie opened her arms and hugged Valerie hard. They held each other for a while as the weight of what was to come settled over them. This change in both of their lives wouldn't be easy, especially for Valerie. She put her heart and soul into this business for nearly twenty years. "So I guess this is it. When am I supposed to leave?"

Valerie pulled back and wiped the tears slipping down her cheeks. "It's best if the two of you leave today. Why keep the wounds open longer than necessary, right?"

Jamie disagreed. She'd love nothing more than to enjoy one final day on this beautiful land before she was forced to leave. But she understood Valerie's reasoning. It was time to go home and form a plan.

After a two-hour flight back to the city, Jamie and Monty shared a taxi downtown.

"Told you she was losing money," Monty said, his voice gruff with resentment.

Jamie stared out the window at the buildings whizzing by as rain pelted the car. Of course the weather suited her miserable mood. "Yeah, well, I don't think either of us expected to be tossed out this fast. I'm really fucked now."

Monty squeezed her shoulder. "You'll be all right, twit."

She turned to him, took in the hard line of his freshly shaved jaw. If she wasn't so upset, she might actually compliment him for finally ditching the porn moustache. "You don't understand. I have nothing, Monty. The money I made this summer is going straight to someone else, and I can't even try to keep it."

His eyes narrowed. "What do you mean?"

The taxi hydroplaned over a puddle before pulling to a heart-pounding stop in front of Monty's apartment building. Jamie stared down at her hands, unsure how to tell him without telling him everything. "You know I haven't always been a good girl."

"Yeah, I know. Jammin' Jamie, right?"

She shook her head, hating that nickname from her drug-induced days. "Well, let's just say that caught up to me before I left for Sharp Ridge." She looked up at him, on the verge of tears. "I'm in a lot of trouble and there's no way out of it."

Monty's expression hardened. "For what? What the hell did you do now?"

The cab driver cleared his throat as Jamie and Monty battled eyeballs at each other. "I can't tell you."

"Listen to me. You can tell me anything, and you know I'm not a saint either." Monty shook his head and dug into his pocket for money. Jamie stared at his profile as he handled the cash, recalling a recent drunken conversation when Monty admitted to robbing a house during a bad moment in his life. Monty and two other men had worn masks and busted into a mansion, only to find the family hadn't yet left for their vacation. Monty was ordered to lock the kids in the room, unaware until it was too late that one of his partners had accidentally shot the father. Monty escaped through a window on the third floor and never looked back. He moved to a new city and started over. He'd lived in his own prison since then, despite trying to put humor into every conversation. Jamie knew of his silent torture, and even though the man had survived the shot, Monty still regretted what happened, because it could've ended up much worse.

Maybe what she did wasn't so bad.

He handed a few bills to the driver. "Make sure she gets home with that." After the cabbie took the cash and rushed to retrieve Monty's hockey bag from the trunk without getting too soaked, her only friend gave her a quick hug. "I'll call you later. I expect you to tell me everything in detail you silly twit." Despite his cruel words, she knew she deserved it. Jamie slouched against the seat, feeling sorry herself as Monty ran up the steps to the building and the cab sped off down the street.

Monty always said the bitter truth—no sugarcoating allowed. Even if she did hate his choice of words at times, she loved his honesty. There weren't many honest folks left in this cruel world.

A few blocks away she exited the cab and headed up the steps to her third-floor studio apartment. If getting laid off and owing a bunch of money to her old dealer wasn't bad enough, seeing an eviction notice on her door had to be the worst news ever. She ripped the note off the door as blinding tears filled her eyes.

You have fourteen days to vacate the premises if all past due rent is not paid in full by end of August. The letter was dated last week, and all rent was due in three days.

The letter dropped to the floor as her knees buckled. Tears slid down her cheeks as her ass connected to the floor. She leaned against the hallway wall and sat there for a long while, unable to form any kind of plan to save herself. It seemed as though her life was slipping through her fingers. In fourteen days she'd be out on the street.

What if she hadn't have come home today? Would the landlord have packed her stuff and thrown it into the street?

Coming up with all past due rent, which totaled over two-thousand dollars, within three days was impossible. Her bank account was overdrawn; she had two grand in cash that was already promised to someone else who would break her legs if she didn't pay up. Her past wasn't a pretty one, but she was an adult and would pay her dues.

She opened her apartment door, dropped her stuff on the floor; kicked her shoes off and into the open hallway closet. Next came the bra. At least she breathed a little easier without the confines of the underwire. On a day like this, that small bit of freedom was a welcome feeling.

After she turned on the radio to her favorite classic rock station, she began to unpack. As she removed her summer gear from her suitcase and duffel bag, Jamie thought she couldn't sink any lower. Once her stuff was put away she went to the kitchen and grabbed her bottle of whiskey—something she always saved for the end of the season. So much for a celebratory drink today. This was a sorrow drinking day. Drink until nothing hurt anymore.

She drank straight out of the bottle. As she took a long swig, she thought of all the things going wrong in her life. A breakup one year ago. Getting fired from her winter job after being accused of stealing when she didn't do it, only to be laid-off from the summer job, was a massive slap in the face. She hadn't had sex in seven months and thirteen days to be precise, and she had three cigarettes left. If she kept the two grand, she'd be broken or worse. Being clean for eight months had its rewards, but now she owed money from a past she wished didn't exist. A past that did nothing but harm her body.

Jamie Fields, get your shit together.

She took the bottle in hand and wandered over to the row of windows overlooking the street. People walked along the sidewalk below her prison of life. They had no idea what she went through. Maybe they were on their way to a fancy dinner when all she found in the freezer was an old forgotten box of fish sticks and a jar of mayo and ketchup in the fridge. Maybe those people were on their way to a family gathering when all she had was her bottle of whiskey. At least she had that.

"Congrats, Jamie. Another wasted day and wasted night for you." She tipped the bottle to her lips and took another long pull.

Her gaze halted on her answering machine as the whiskey burnt a path down her throat. Six messages. Messages she didn't want to hear. Probably more bill collectors or maybe a death threat.

She couldn't help it. She burst out in hysterical laughter, followed by a wretched sob. "Why me?!" she screamed.

Her neighbor pounded on the wall. "Keep it down!"

Ugh. She plopped down onto the couch and stared blankly at her surroundings.

The tiny apartment of four-hundred square feet had a kitchenette with a three-burner stove and mini fridge beneath. No table. No chairs. A bed on one side, a dresser with television on the other, and a loveseat at the foot of the bed. She might as well be living in a boarding house, but at least she had her own bathroom.

All this splendor for eight-hundred dollars per month, she thought with a bitter taste in her mouth. And now she didn't even have cable or Internet. She closed her eyes and tried to think of nice things. Card games and fishing on the lake. Giving Monty a hard time. Shore lunches and fishing. Good things that made her happy. Now she couldn't even afford a pack of cigarettes.

Not so long ago, she would've found a way to buy a bag and forget her troubles. To take life through a straw and snort her cares away. But she wasn't that person any more. She had to be tough, take it day by day, and never look back. Never ever look back.

With all this horror swimming in her head, she finished the bottle of whiskey and fell into a drunken sleep on the loveseat.

* * * *

The next morning Jamie was startled awake by the phone ringing. She pushed up to a sitting position on the couch and looked around in a confused haze. Her eyes felt like sandpaper, her head felt like a watermelon, and her mouth tasted like an ashtray. It took a moment to realize she was back at home and not at Sharp Ridge Lodge where it was safe. Being back home didn't feel real. It seemed like a demented dream, and maybe, if she blinked harder, she would wake up at Sharp Ridge in her small comfy cabin, with the potbellied stove in the middle of the floor—the only place that felt like home.

She pushed up from the couch and ran to the phone, surprised it still worked since she owed the phone company money as well. Still groggy from sleep, and the whiskey, she answered in a ragged tone, "Hello?"

"Get up, twit. I have a job that might help your little situation."

Jamie glared at the phone as if Monty could see it. How he could sound so lively this early in the morning should be a crime. "Does it involve cleaning toilets?" She leaned against the kitchen counter and rubbed her forehead, hoping that would clear away the watermelon seeds clogging her brain. "Hello?"

"I made a few phone calls last night. If you care to hear the details, then I suggest you get your sweet ass dressed and meet me around the corner at our favorite coffee shop. Unless you'd like to go to the bar instead?"

Jamie gagged. "God no. I had enough last night."

"I thought so. Get dressed and meet me at noon. This has to be said in person." He hung up before Jamie could respond. She put the cordless back on the charger and nearly laughed out loud with excitement. Maybe this was it. Maybe he had a job prospect that could get her out of this mess.

As Jamie walked to her dresser, feeling relieved that something positive might finally happen, the apartment door burst open and slammed against the wall. She spun around and screamed as two burly men stormed inside her apartment. The one holding the baseball bat went straight to her television and smashed it to pieces. The other man rushed her, pinned her against the wall by her throat, and said through clenched teeth, "That will be your legs in two days if you don't give Jones his money by then."

She had no words, no breath as he released her throat and backed away.

On the way out the door, the man with the baseball bat busted the drywall on both sides of the hallway. Every hit made her body jerk. As their bulky frames disappeared out the door and down the steps as fast as they broke in, Jamie slunk down the wall and burst into wretched sobs.

How could she pay Jones in two days and pay her landlord as well? Maybe she should pack a bag and disappear with the cash she had, start fresh in a new town where nobody knew her. But Jones would find her. He had a long arm, and every shady character in this country knew him well.

She hugged her knees and lowered her forehead to her lap, wishing something good could come her way.

A creak in the floor made her look up. Mrs. Watson, the elderly lady from next door, stood in the middle of the room looking at the damage, her eyes wide. "What happened here?"

Jamie took a deep breath, dried her eyes, and pushed up to her feet. "Nothing you need to worry about. I'm sorry you had to hear that."

Mrs. Watson glanced at her now, her expression full of concern. "Should I call the police?"

"No. No. Please don't," Jamie begged. "I'll have this fixed. I promise. It was just a misunderstanding with a friend. No need to worry about it."

Mrs. Watson clucked her tongue. "I think you need to change your friends." She took one last look through the room, turned around, and headed back out the door, mumbling under her breath, "Damn young people are gonna give me a heart attack...."

Jamie went to the door. Even though the frame was cracked and splinters of wood lay scattered across the floor, she was still able to close it. That was a small comfort at least, even though she knew they could burst back in anytime they wanted.

She quickly dressed, her mind racing on how she could get out of this mess that was veering out of control. If she had a choice, she would've stayed at Sharp Ridge and never came back.

Right at noon, Jamie walked into the coffee shop around the corner. Monty stood and smiled, but his expression hardened as his intent gaze took in her defeated expression. As she approached the table, she knew her eyes were swollen and red from crying. She tried her best to hide it but she couldn't be strong any more—not after her visit less than an hour before.

Monty came around the table and wrapped her up in his arms, rubbing her hair as she sobbed against his chest.

"This is it, Monty. I'm really fucked. Jones's boys busted into my place right after you called me."

Monty let out a hard sigh. "I thought you quit hanging with him."

"I did!" She wiped her eyes on his T-shirt. "I've been clean for eight months. But I"—she stepped back and pulled out a chair from the table—"I borrowed large and I was ripped off."

He glared at her as he took his seat opposite hers. "Big mistake. Especially with Jones. How long did he give you to pay up?"

"Two days."

"How much?"

"Twenty-five hundred. That's more than what I earned so far this summer, and I owe my landlord money, too."

His eyebrows lifted high as he shook his head in disbelief. "That's no small amount. He's broken legs for a lot less."

"I'm an idiot. I could give Jones what I have—even though there's still more—but then I'd still owe the landlord. I don't know what to do!" And even if Monty offered to take her in, he already had a roommate in tight quarters. She had nowhere else to go, aside from the women's shelter, and she had too much pride for that. There had to be something she could do. Anything that didn't involve selling herself on the street.

"I've been calling you a twit for a reason." Monty waved a waitress over and ordered espressos for both of them. "How about a slice of pie? It's lemon. Isn't that your favorite?"

Bless his heart for remembering her sweet tooth. Jamie wanted to kiss him and slap him for being so generous. Must be nice to have money to spend even after getting laid off. Maybe she should ask Monty to buy her a pack of smokes. She sucked her last one back in under a minute on the way here. "Sure. Thanks."

When the waitress left to fill their order, Monty stared at Jamie for a long minute. "If I had the money, I'd give it to you. But as it is I'm hard up as well."

Jamie lowered her gaze to the table top. "I know." Having only known her for five years his generosity choked her up, even if he wasn't able to help. The offer alone made him a good friend in her books, and she would do the same for him without hesitation if their roles were reversed.

"But I brought you here because I have a proposition. When was the last time you had a vacation?"

Jamie blinked in surprise at the unexpected question. "Uh, I went camping at Algonquin Park a couple of years ago. Why?"

He tipped his head back and released a throaty laugh. "That isn't a vacation."

Jamie sighed. His comment made her feel really low. "I like the bush."

"I know, but I mean a real vacation. Somewhere tropical. A place with white sand beaches and music in the night. Sexy cabana boys to serve you." He waggled his eyebrows.

Jamie couldn't imagine ever being lucky enough to get that. The waitress arrived with their order and Jamie almost groaned aloud over her first bite of the pie. "This is awesome." Almost as good as an orgasm. A vision of that Jack guy flashed through her mind. She almost blushed at the memory of how his hard body felt against hers. Too much time had passed since she'd felt the warmth of a man.

Monty took a sip of his espresso, watching Jamie carefully. He had yet to touch his pie. "Let's get down to it, then. I got through to an old friend who needs someone to go to Cuba—"

"Cuba?" Her hand holding the fork stilled over the pie. "Are you serious? For what?"

Monty's expression remained the same—determined. "Agree to go and I'll give you the details."

Jamie set her fork down and regarded him seriously. "Look, Cuba sounds awesome but I'm about to get evicted from my apartment, have my legs and possibly my face broken, and I'm way behind on bills. Taking off on a trip isn't happening. Not now, and maybe not ever."

Monty leaned closer, still undeterred. "All expenses will be paid, and you'll even get paid to go."

Get paid to go on a free vacation? Jamie frowned. This sounded too good to be true. "What's the catch?"

Monty shook his head quickly. "Nothing. Just go to Havana and meet up with my friend's contact who lives there." This time Monty couldn't seem to look Jamie straight in the eye, and that worried her more than anything.

"Meet with your friend's contact? This is beginning to sound like a drug deal and you want me to be a mule or something. I'm sorry, but I'm not going to jail for a free vacation, Monty. That side of my life was over a long time ago."

Monty sat forward and shook his head hard. "No drugs involved, I promise. I'd go myself but I can't."

"Why not?"

"Because my new job starts on Friday, and it's at a classy new restaurant. This is a once-in-a-lifetime opportunity for me." He averted his attention to the view outside. Jamie gave him a sharp, speculative glance as Monty struggled to say more. It seemed as if he was afraid of something. "The date of the trip can't be changed, and she paid a lot of money for this to happen. She put her trust in me, and I trust you." He shrugged. "Works for me."

Jamie eyed him suspiciously. "Who is she?"

He chuckled, at himself it seemed, then glanced out the window. "We met on a job a long time ago. Tough girl. Smart. Beautiful...."

Jamie suspected there had been more to them than a job. "So why aren't you with her since you're obviously still infatuated?"

Monty blew out a sharp breath. "She fell in love with somebody else. Somebody with a lot more money and connections."

The hardened tone of his voice made Jamie even more suspicious of this mission. "Then why are you talking to her now?"

Monty stared directly at Jamie, his jaw tight, shoulders stiff. "Because I owe her a favor, and I want to help you. I called her up to see if she had any jobs. I would've taken it and gave you the money."

Jamie sighed hard. Her throat felt tight. Why couldn't she love this man more than a friend? She wanted to be happy, and she wanted Monty to be happy. Still, it didn't make sense to go on a trip in someone else's place, all for a package. "Why can't she just change the date or ship the package?"

"Because she can't go and the package can't be shipped. Look, I know this might seem strange"—he leaned forward and placed his hand over Jamie's forearm—"but I trust you. And since you're going through a difficult time, I thought you might enjoy this trip, and you need the money pretty badly. And I can't tell you who she is—she wants to remain anonymous."

Jamie stared down at his hand on her arm before she looked back up and tried to read Monty's expression. His big blues were full of hope and trust, and it almost made her cave in then and there. *Almost.* This whole thing didn't seem right. But she was desperate. What else could she possibly do aside from selling her body to get out of debt? "What's in the package?"

Monty sat back in his seat, his eyes glinting with an emotion Jamie couldn't read. "I don't know, to be honest. What I do know is that it revolves around some organization or whatever, and it's very important."

Jamie leaned back and blew out a frustrated breath. She wasn't sure where to go with this. On one hand, she could be smart and just say no.

On the other, the prospect of a free trip and earning some money could be exactly what she needed. "If I get arrested, I swear to God I'll kill you."

Monty chuckled, not at all put off by her words. "Even if you did have to return with something—which you won't—private jets and private airstrips don't question anyone about anything. You could bring a dead body back home with you and no one would lift a brow."

She thought hard for a moment but couldn't come up with a smart remark. "This just sounds weird. So I go to Cuba to deliver a package. Just like that? That's it?"

Monty shrugged. "Sort of."

"What do you mean sort of? You better explain to me what the hell is going on here. You're putting me at risk, you know." She sucked in a deep, calming breath. "I may be desperate, Monty, but I'm not stupid."

"I know." Monty sighed and leaned forward, elbows on table. "You'll be going there with a package in exchange for another. Like a trade, really. Once you have it, you'll meet up with her contact and deliver it. That's it."

"So I won't be returning with anything? Just delivering one package in exchange for another, and handing that off, too?"

"Exactly."

That didn't sound too painful, but she still had a sinking suspicion that drugs were involved. She stared down at the table as fear and desperation warred in her mind. A long time ago she promised herself never to get caught up in that again. "You know what's in the package, don't you?"

"I swear I don't." Monty stood and set a piece of paper on the table that listed a phone number. "When you make your decision, call this number. Whatever you decide, don't share this number with anyone."

As Monty walked past the table, Jamie grabbed his forearm, halting him. "You said I'd get paid to go on a vacation. How much are we talking about?"

"Fifty thousand."

"Dollars?" *Holy shit.* Jamie blinked hard. "That's a lot of money on top of a free vacation." She thought hard for a second. *This could be very good, or totally against everything I promised never to do again.* "If I agree to go, would I get the money before or after the trip?"

He grinned as if he knew she would say yes. "Half before, the other half when the final exchange is done. Sounds fair, right?"

Jamie nodded and released his arm. Monty leaned closer and added, "You don't have to do this, Jamie. But if you do, within a week all of your worries will be over. Just think about it."

As her only friend walked away and pushed the door to the coffee shop open, he said over his shoulder, "You have twenty-four hours to decide," and walked out the door.

Later that night Jamie paced her apartment. As crazy as Monty's offer sounded, she couldn't help but think about it all night. That much money would get her out of debt, even though she knew there was something shifty about it. She could pay her landlord and Jones with the first payment and still be laughing. She could rest easy knowing she had some money while still finding a job—with a roof over her head and food in her stomach.

What do I have to lose by doing this? "Possibly my pride, my freedom, or even my life," she said aloud.

She stared at the only picture hanging in her apartment—a view of the bay at Sharp Ridge Lodge. What would Cuba be like compared to the lodge? Like night and day, she imagined. A deep tissue massage versus hard work. Having someone else take care of her versus cleaning someone else's bathroom. A walk on a soft, sandy beach rather than a rocky shoreline. A sexy cabana boy to serve her drinks instead of making them herself. *Huh.* The idea was sounding slightly better every minute.

But what if this was some sick joke by a woman she didn't even know? Monty may trust this person, but how could she? Obviously this anonymous woman had money. Jamie, on the other hand, had two days to pay a dangerous debt, and fourteen days until she was homeless.

Monty would never steer me in the wrong direction.

She was utterly hopeless if she didn't take this job. But she had until noon tomorrow to make up her mind. On impulse, Jamie grabbed her fall coat from the hallway closet and took off for a long walk to clear her head.

It was just past midnight as she crested the hill that overlooked the waterfront, a few blocks from her apartment building. Five cargo ships were lined up in the bay, as still and soundless as a painting over the placid water. The view was incredible from here. The lights from the boats twinkled over the water connecting to the lights from the shipping lanes at shore. They all waited to be docked come morning and filled with the grains from the terminals.

Some might think of this industrial view as ugly, but Jamie thought it was beautiful—especially at night when all was quiet, when no traffic or people or seagulls disturbed the scene. The darkness of night always held a certain appeal to her since she was a kid. During the darker moments of her life, she would close her eyes and imagine something good. Nighttime had the same appeal. She could be anyone at night. Anyone she wanted to be.

When Jamie finally returned home, she picked up the phone and dialed the number despite the crude hour.

A sleepy, feminine voice answered. "Yes?"

"This is Jamie, Monty's friend. I thought about the offer."

"And?"

She took a deep breath. "When do I leave?"

Chapter 4

Sam rolled up the sleeves of his navy blue Guayabera shirt and leaned over the balcony on the rooftop terrace. It was midmorning in Old Havana and already over thirty degrees. Once again he was shipped off to a beautiful place that he wouldn't be able to enjoy, not in the true sense, all because some greedy woman was blackmailing them for ten-million bucks.

He wanted all of this to be over. Sure, he'd take a contract here and there to pay the bills, but anything to do with the McCoys should no longer involve business of an illegal nature. Terry made sure of that. He stepped off the podium and gave his blessing to Antonio Montesano to do whatever he desired. They were done. The McCoy Empire was nothing but a memory, and a crazy one at that. Now that Terry had sold the family estate at Saanich Inlet, he was now considering moving out of the hotel penthouse in Victoria and buying into the suburban life. It would be better for the children.

Sam thought his brother was really becoming a sap. He couldn't imagine a woman being able to do that; turning him into a wimpy excuse of a man. Gabe, on the other hand, still remained the same. Sam knew the change in lifestyle would be harder for him, because Gabe was more like Sam with a take-it-or-leave-it mentality.

He wiped the sweat from his brow and withdrew the tin cigarette case from the lower pocket of his shirt. As he flipped open the case and pulled out a cigarette, he remembered buying the silver trinket at a shop in Switzerland four years past, on a job that nearly killed him. All because a little boy walked out onto the wrong street at the wrong time. He jumped in front and took a bullet for that boy. He didn't regret his decision for one second, even though his target had gotten away and killed another. That boy meant life to him in that split second, and he'd take life over death any day of the year.

As he inhaled the pungent smoke, reminiscing of his life spent in the grip of danger, he went over the recent information Terry had given him before Sam left Victoria. A transaction was to be made the day after tomorrow at exactly 5 p.m. In exchange for the money, the woman would hand over all physical proof she had about the McCoys and their business dealings. Hundreds of photographs. Tape recordings. Video surveillance. They were all in deep without a leg to stand on. Even their friends in the police department couldn't help them now. Not when some of them were included with this shady deal. Hell, even a few judges were in deep.

Lives were at stake, and Sammy Hayes would be the one to save them all. He wouldn't let them down, and he wouldn't let Auntie Rose down either, no matter if he took his last breath seeing it to the end.

It worried Sam how this woman managed to get all of this information without getting caught. Someone must have given it to her, but who? Everyone had been paid off or snuffed out. Nothing else made any sense. Even when the boys had a brief fling with a woman in the past, she was never told any details about the business.

But then there was the little matter of discovering last year that Colton's second wife, Wanda—or Daniella, as they had learned later on—the eldest daughter of Antonio Montesano, had known a great deal about the business. Colton had allowed her to be a part of his meetings, and she even made some business decisions for him while he was away. When Colton became suspicious of her, he'd called upon Sam to be a pawn—to get close to her by any means necessary—and make her trust him. But sometimes getting close to the other sex leads to uncontrollable feelings. Sam didn't want to like Wanda, and he sure as hell didn't want to grow fond of her, yet he did. She'd twisted his mind and heart into believing that he had meant something to her, and in the end, she tried to have him killed anyway.

If Sam hadn't have accepted that role, and seen it to the end, they all could've been killed.

Perhaps Wanda wanted revenge for Terry sending her back to her controlling father. She knew enough to cause hell for all of them, but Sam didn't think she was that stupid to seek revenge on something she knew she deserved. They could've killed her, but they didn't, and now that her father was in control of the syndicate, he'd make damn sure she didn't cause trouble. Still, Sam would keep his eyes peeled in case he saw her. If she showed up here, then he knew it had be her.

Whatever the case may be, Sam knew what must be done. Once the woman met Gabe and the exchange was made, Sam would follow her to make sure she was in this alone, and then kill her. That was the arrangement only the boys knew about. It was the only way to keep them all safe.

He checked his watch. Gabe should be arriving any minute at his hotel a few blocks over. They would meet briefly to get the details hashed out, then go on their merry way until Gabe made the exchange. Sam would finish the job on his own.

From his position on the rooftop terrace, he took in the bustling view of the pedestrian street below. There were fewer tourists this time of year during hurricane season, but that still didn't stop many who did dare venture at this time. Locals filled the streets on their day-to-day errands. The blistering sun shone like a beacon in the sky, yet it barely illuminated the narrow streets that weaved between clusters of old buildings.

So far there had been no signs of a storm brewing, and with a beautiful day like this, everyone was out and about.

Stunning architecture surrounded him. Rooftop terraces spanned as far as he could see. Flowering vines in every color climbed crumbling walls. The Malecón, the seaside avenue that runs along the seawall at Havana Port, was a five-minute walk away, yet from here he could see the stunning ocean clearly.

He loved it here. Loved this hotel especially. Sam wasn't sure exactly why he loved Havana—even though he barely got to enjoy it—there was something about the diverse culture that made him feel at home. He could be invisible here, but he'd also made a few friends.

Behind him a family of five chatted over dinner. A few tables away a young couple shared drinks, oblivious to everyone else around them. A table of rowdy men boasted over their adventures from the night before, into their cups again, all while a small group of servers stood by to be called upon.

It was his job to know what was around him. What details meant life or death. It was during his recon of the place when he noticed her.

She sat at the bar with her back to him, her blond hair in a messy twist atop her head. A few loose strands trickled down her neck and over her bare upper back. It made him think of water curving around pebbles in a creek bed. Sam gave her a thorough once-over, taking in the curvy frame donned in a breezy white summer dress. He noted a purple tattoo on the back of her tanned left shoulder—some type of flower, he imagined—but couldn't make out the whole of it beneath the strap of her dress. His gaze traveled down, all the way to her small feet clad in sandals, one hooked over the bottom cross bar of her stool, one lying on the terrace floor beneath her. For a moment he thought of going over and striking up a conversation, maybe handing her the lost sandal, but thought better of it. She was probably waiting for her husband, or maybe a secret lover. Havana had to be the capitol of great love affairs.

He turned back to his view of the street and pushed the woman from his mind. He had work to do. There was no time for fun with ten million at stake. Besides, women were everywhere on these narrow streets. She was just one of thousands in every shape and color to look at. Tomorrow when his job was done, only then could he have a night of fun before he had to leave.

"Would you care for another drink, sir?"

Sam glanced over his shoulder and smiled at the server. "I'm fine, thank you."

As the young man turned away, Sam's gaze fixed on the lone woman again as she got off the stool and squatted down to pick up her sandal. He stared, tapped like metal to a magnet, as she slipped the dainty sandal onto her tiny foot. From his stance less than fifteen feet away, he noted she had the kind of cute feet that made a man want to kiss them…then work his way up, right to the heart of the matter.

And then she turned around.

Holy fuck. Sam quickly spun around and sucked in a sharp breath.

The housekeeper. Sharp Ridge Lodge. *What the hell?*

Sam's heart pounded as he tried to lean casually against the railing and not catch her attention. She must not have seen him yet, which was a good thing, because he wouldn't know what to say. He'd never been tongue-tied before in his life. Ever.

That night on the dock rushed through his mind. How her soft, smooth voice washed over him like a sweet cocktail. How her warm lips crushed against his for a kiss that rocked him to the core. He was startled how her presence affected him. He was even more affected that she was here at this precise time.

"Thank you so much. What a wonderful place," he heard her say to the bartender. A vision of Wanda came to mind. How she'd lured him into a whirlwind of sex and chaos—even though it was his job to get close to her—only to be betrayed by the wicked witch in the end. Maybe they were all the same.

Sam wondered if Jamie was staying here or if she had stumbled upon this quaint terrace bar by chance. Or did she know who he was and followed him here? Anything could be possible when it came to females.

What were the odds that the strange woman he had kissed under the stars in Northern Canada was the same woman in his hotel, in Cuba?

He counted sixty seconds in his head and discreetly glanced over his shoulder. She had already disappeared inside toward the interior stairwell. He took another drag of his smoke, put it out in a nearby ashtray, and followed her.

As the woman who had tormented his dreams this past week exited the hotel and weaved through the narrow streets, Sam kept his distance but never let her out of his sight. When she stopped at a bookshop, he paused a short distance away and blended in with the ever-present crowd. When she was offered a taxi, he stopped to stare into a shop window.

Naturally suspicious, Sam concluded that this Jamie broad, a so-called housekeeper at a wilderness lodge, could very well be the woman he was after. This was way too much of a coincidence that she was here, right now, at the same time as Sam during a ten-million-dollar blackmail. With his curiosity and his instinct piqued, he continued to follow her every move, even several hours later when she returned to her hotel room. As much as he'd like to relax over a few drinks, his work was never really done.

Once she ascended the stairs to the upper floors, he immediately went to the front desk. The cute young lady smiled as he leaned onto the counter and fixed her with a grin that would make the lips in her panties flutter. "Good evening. That scarf matches your eyes perfectly. Is it silk?"

She blushed and cleared her throat nervously. "Yes, thank you."

He made a show of glancing at the stairs and chuckled. "See that blonde that just walked away from me?" At her nod, he continued. "I'm afraid she's upset with me on our first date, and left with the only key to our room. Would you be so kind and give me a second one? I'd hate to have to rent another room when I plan to make it up to her. Apologizing can be fun and very rewarding."

Her knowing smile was all he needed to see. He had her hooked. "Of course, sir."

"Jamie is her name, although I'm afraid we haven't gotten major details sorted out yet…if you know what I mean."

She tapped away at the keyboard. "Ah, yes, here she is. Jamie Fields of room 312." She slipped a key card through the machine, punched in the room number, and handed it to him. "There you go, sir. Have a wonderful night making it up to her."

Sam accepted the card with a smile, winked, and walked around the corner out of her view, and left through a side door. He had some surveillance to do first.

The sun was beginning to set as Sam settled into a small niche on the rooftop of the building directly across from the hotel. He withdrew his binoculars and retrieved his cell from his pocket to dial Gabe. Sweat beaded down the back of his neck.

A raspy voice answered on the second ring. "Hey, shitstick," Gabe said with all seriousness.

"Fucktard." Sam chuckled. "I have some interesting news. Care for a look-see with your favorite brother?" He gave precise directions and waited for Gabe to arrive as the housekeeper settled into her room.

A short while later he shifted from one cheek to the other to get the feeling back in his ass as he continued with his surveillance. The nightlife had just begun on day one of the mission.

Miss Jamie Fields of room 312 had just stepped out of the bathroom with a towel wrapped around her body and another twisted around her hair. Years of experience taught Sam not to get worked up over a half-naked woman—especially one with secrets. Secrets that could ruin them all.

Maybe Jamie wasn't even her real name, which would be expected for a liar. Hell, Sam had to use fake names quite often to preserve his identity and his life, as he had used Jack Daniels during his vacation at Sharp Ridge Lodge.

"There you are, you skinny prick." Sam looked up as Gabe crested the narrow stone staircase leading to the rooftop, and walked toward him, his face and his body language expressing complete boredom. "What's so exciting you want me to meet you on a private rooftop? Did you suddenly switch sides?"

Sam glanced up at Gabe and gave him a saucy wink. He laughed under his breath over his brother's unsettled expression. "I wouldn't switch for you, believe me." He handed Gabe his binoculars and moved to the side of the niche. "Third floor, fourth window to your right. Tell me what you see."

After a minute of surveillance, Gabe glanced at Sam and raised a brow. "We've resorted to spying on naked women now?"

"What?" Sam ripped the binocs from Gabe's hand and stared hard at the view.

Through the billowing sheer curtains he noted every detail as she stood there completely naked in the middle of the room. *Jesus Christ.* It wasn't his motto to watch a woman in a vulnerable state when she wasn't aware, but something made him stare at her as if it was his mission in life. He watched everything, from how she lifted one foot onto the mattress and massaged some type of lotion onto her shapely leg. He swallowed. Each deft stroke seemed to reach right into his pants and grip him hard. As she finished the other leg and proceeded to rub the lotion in other delicate areas, he decided that he missed the company of a woman. If he were to be honest with himself, he'd admit he wouldn't mind *her* company.

Her breasts were large and her hips curvy. He liked that she a little extra meat on her bones. To him that was a real woman. Nobody wants to cuddle with a stick after all. Minutes passed as he watched in rapt fascination, appreciating every little detail, yet tortured by her natural beauty.

"You do realize I'm married now, right?"

He nearly jumped, having forgotten Gabe was beside him. "Yeah."

The look in Gabe's eyes should be directed at a child—not at a grown-ass man who could kill him up close and personal, or at a distance. "Don't tell me you picked up this broad and now you need my approval?"

"Nope."

"Then why am I here? I'd rather be on the phone with my wife then on a rooftop staring at a naked woman like some desperate, virgin brat."

Sam lowered the binocs and glared at him. "I'm not a virgin and I'm definitely not desperate. Brat, well…."

Gabe stared at him in disbelief then shook his head. "You're fucked."

"Not yet. Although I wouldn't mind—"

"Shut up and be serious."

He sighed and cut the comedy act. "I met her a week ago at a resort in Northern Ontario. Now she's here. Doesn't that seem a little coincidental to you?"

Gabe's expression turned hard. He grabbed the binocs back and stared at the room again. "You think it could be her? I've never seen her before in my life, and I don't see a briefcase in the room, or anything else that makes her look like anything but a tourist. Could be a coincidence."

"I'm not taking any chances."

After a moment of recon, Gabe handed the binocs back. "So what's the plan?"

"Tuesday evening you're going to meet the woman at that outdoor café I told you about. She'll be wearing a red dress, carrying a black briefcase, and a book about crocheting."

"Really? Crocheting? Your aunt really did a number on you, didn't she?"

He shrugged. "I thought it would be a nice touch. Anyway, if something changes, then I'll call you." Sam shooed him away. "Go call your wife now, you prick. I'll see you later."

Gabe slugged him in the shoulder. Sam grimaced and rubbed the sore spot, glaring at Gabe's back as he walked toward the stairs. "By the way, you look ridiculous. Miami Vice called, they want their suit back." Gabe's chuckle faded as he disappeared down the steps.

As any good man should do on surveillance, Sam kept a keen eye on the woman. It didn't matter that she was naked, but he adjusted his seat again and cleared his throat, completely uncomfortable with the tightness of his slacks. He tried to focus on her belongings, particularly if she had a briefcase in the room. Vacationers never traveled with briefcases unless they were filled with money—or documents that could ruin lives. But Gabe was right, he didn't see anything suspicious. If she was simply a business woman, which he knew she wasn't, then she would appear businesslike—not carefree like a random college girl out for a good time. The more he thought about it, the more he wasn't so sure.

An hour passed as Miss Fields wandered leisurely about her room. She took her time slipping on a light and silky-looking nightgown. Even though he was glad she had covered up, he could clearly see her nipples through the garment. Then she sat on the edge of the bed and brushed her hair for what felt like an eternity.

Sam yawned, becoming bored with the recon and tired from staring through binoculars for so long. He set them down and leaned against the stone wall to take a calming breath and rest his eyes. He didn't expect to see her today, and he sure as hell didn't expect to be this troubled by her.

While Gabe and Terry had previously dated bad girls, but fell in love with good ones, Sam had always been attracted to the good girls. He didn't want anything to do with a woman who didn't have passion for life and love in her heart, and an honest bone in her body.

He thought that Jamie was one of those good girls when he met her at the lodge. Now he wasn't so sure. He had no proof that she was the one he was after, but there was only one way to find out....

* * * *

Day two of the mission and Jamie was in paradise.

A busy car-honking and exhaust-fuming taxi ride took her to Santa Maria, the western side of the ten-kilometer beach at Playa del Este. Clutching her beach bag and wearing a breezy cover over her bikini, she walked out onto the beach and wanted to scream and laugh out loud. The view of the endless white sand and vast ocean was breathtaking. *Nothing compares to this.*

The air was hot, the breeze balmy, and the sway of the palms a short distance behind created an atmosphere no town back home could offer. In less than twenty-four hours she decided that she didn't want to go home. Why not complete the mission and just stay here and spend all that money?

It was a thought worth considering since she had nothing left to return to anyway, aside from no job prospects and loneliness.

Feeling carefree and exhilarated in this foreign place, she found a spot away from the hustle of the crowd to place her towel on the sand. Next she removed her bikini cover and lounged back in sweet, tropical bliss.

The sound of the waves sloshing against the sandy shore, and the heat of the sun, was more calming than any boat ride at Sharp Ridge Lodge, she had to admit. She shielded her eyes and stared at a family having a picnic close by. A little girl wearing a red-and-white polka dot bathing suit grabbed a handful of sand and whipped it up in the air. She squealed in delight as the sand came back down, pelting her head and shoulders.

Jamie smiled, wishing she could feel free like that little girl.

After an hour of people watching and sunbathing, Jamie drifted off in a heat-induced sleep. Sometime later she woke up with a start as something tapped against her foot. She opened her eyes and was shocked to see that clouds had covered the sun and the wind had whipped several lounging chairs across the beach.

She pushed up on her elbows and looked around. Only a few people remained on the beach, and they were gathering their things and getting ready to head out. Parents yelled after their children. Baskets and towels and chairs were gathered quickly. Waves crashed against the shore, bouncing a few water toys that were left behind.

Shocked that the weather could change so quickly, Jamie gathered her things and headed to the nearest hotel to order a taxi back into town.

With her hair in disarray and sand stuck between her toes, she arrived safely back at her hotel in the middle of Old Havana, just in time as the wind battered against the building. The shutters in the lobby and piano bar were closed. The lights flickered, but a few locals and hotel guests remained in the lounge, mingling and enjoying drinks as she made her way up to her room to change.

When she had first arrived at her hotel yesterday afternoon, she thought she had walked into the wrong place. The hotel had a salmon-pink exterior with Spanish colonial details and a live piano bar for a lobby. This old world city on the ocean with its numerous old buildings and narrow streets was a far cry from any place she had seen before.

She wandered the hotel before heading into her room, taking in the character with rapt fascination. She'd never been anywhere before with such historical detail. She also visited the famous suite where tourists could view the very room where Ernest Hemingway had lived for several years. The room had been left as if the famous writer might have left it during his stay in the 1930s. She'd also noticed several photographs dedicated to him in the lobby.

She had just finished a hot shower and was brushing her hair when she heard a knock at the door.

"Who is it?" She grabbed the robe provided by the hotel, slipped it on, and stepped quietly to the door to listen. She didn't expect a visitor on her second day here.

"I have a message from the front desk," said a muffled voice.

After checking the peephole, she unlocked and opened the door. Perhaps Monty's friend had new orders for her and didn't want to risk calling up to the room.

"Here you go, ma'am." The bellhop handed her a sealed envelope. "The man requested that you read it right away." The servant waited patiently as Jamie tore open the envelope and read the note.

Come to the lobby. There is no time to wait.

Jamie's heart tripped and her breath hitched in her lungs as she reread the words. "Who sent this?"

The servant shook his head. "I don't know, Miss. I was only following orders to deliver it to this room right away."

A terrified yet exciting thrill rushed through her as she leaned out of the door and stared around the central balcony which looked down through all floors. Nobody else was in sight. Still, Jamie couldn't manage to keep her hands from shaking or calm the savage expression on her face when she glanced back at the young man. "Did you see who it was?"

Again the servant shook his head. "No, Miss. But there was a man dressed in a business suit and carrying a briefcase at the counter when I was sent up here, if that helps."

"Thank you." She rushed back into the room, slamming the door behind her. In three minutes she managed to whip on a pair of jeans, a T-shirt, and grab the briefcase. Rushing like a madman, she grabbed her key card, blew out the door, and rushed down the stairs. Maybe he was still there. Maybe she could make the exchange now and be able to relax until the second and final exchange.

That note scared her half to death. She felt threatened by it, and she had nobody to turn to for advice. Besides, she couldn't risk telling anyone why she was really here, even when she didn't really know what she was delivering.

She blew into the lobby like a lunatic. Several people who were gathered on the couches in the lobby stared as if she had escaped an institution. She slowed her frantic pace and took a deep breath, plastered a smile on her face, and tried to appear collected. The man wearing a business suit and carrying a briefcase was nowhere to be found.

Jamie walked up to the front desk and leaned heavily against it, her heart still hammering. "Did a man just come here looking for me?"

The receptionist blinked hard. "I'm not sure who you are, *Señora*."

"Jamie. Jamie Fields. I'm staying in room 312," she said in a low voice, and quickly looked over her shoulder.

The woman checked her computer and shook her head. "I'm sorry, but there's no record," she said, her accent lilting with every word. "I don't know what message was sent through the previous shift."

Ugh. "Okay. Thank you." Jamie walked away from the front desk. As she started back for the stairs, she paused when a scary-looking woman came to her attention. She nearly jumped back in horror when she realized it was her own reflection in a large mirror. Her hair looked like a mangrove, she hadn't put on her bra, and when she looked down, she realized she was barefoot. No wonder everyone stared at her as if she'd lost her sanity somewhere.

Heading up the stairs, her nerves still frayed, she decided to stick with the original plan of meeting at the outdoor café tomorrow. She didn't want to screw this up. If the guy wanted to make the exchange now, that was fine by her, as long as it was done and everything went smoothly.

"Jamie? Is that you?"

That voice. That whiskey-flavored baritone could only belong to one man.

She jerked around; a hot flush crept up her neck; her back and the briefcase collided with the stairwell. She blinked hard, completely startled and bewildered to see the handsome face that matched the riveting voice.

"Jack! Oh, my, I…. W-what are you doing here?" Her heart pounded furiously and her hand trembled as his gaze shifted from the suitcase back to her face.

"I should ask you the same," he said, his eyes wide, mouth set in a grim line, as if he was concerned for her. "Are you okay? You seem…startled."

"Uh, yes"—she shook her head—"I mean…no." She sucked in a deep breath and tried to calm herself. She had no idea what to say to him. That night on the dock tore through her mind, leaving her embarrassed and thoroughly unprepared to face him. She moved away from the wall and hid the briefcase behind her.

"I just happened to be in the piano bar," he added. "I couldn't believe my eyes when I saw your face." His gaze traveled down, and Jamie's cheeks burned when she realized he was staring at her braless tits. His intent stare made her nipples jerk into tight little buds. *Not now, you little bastards.* His gaze darted back up and he cleared his throat. "I'm blown away to see you here. Why aren't you at the lodge?"

"Uh, well, it's actually a long story." She tried hard not to sound nervous, especially when his presence made her feel like an unraveled ball of yarn.

"Is everything all right? You seem a little out of it."

"Well, I....There was some confusion with reception. I received a call to come down immediately, but apparently it was...for someone else." She forced herself to keep eye contact.

He seemed skeptical by her answer. "Ah." He nodded, and shoved his hands into the pockets of his slacks. "Well then. Would you care to join me for a nightcap in the piano bar?" He shifted on his feet, either uncomfortable with their odd conversation or maybe her disheveled appearance. Whatever the case, Jamie wanted to die of embarrassment. "If you're not doing anything else?"

Should she have a drink with him? As much as it thrilled her to see him here, she wasn't sure if it would be smart to mingle with a man when she had an important mission to carry out. But maybe a companion was exactly what she needed. He may be a stranger—a very sexy stranger—but at least she knew him enough not to feel so alone in this place far away from home. Of course, she couldn't tell him everything, but at least she knew somebody around here. If she ran into trouble, maybe Jack could help her. She offered a smile, pushing aside her worries of tomorrow. "Okay. Sure. Can you give me a few minutes to get ready? I just got out of the shower when I was interrupted."

He returned her smile, his gaze once again on her chest. "Absolutely. I'll be waiting for you down here in the piano bar." His intent stare finally returned to her eyes. "No need to rush. I must admit it's nice to see you again."

Jamie released the breath she'd been holding and forced a winning smile. The way he looked at her as if it was a lot more than nice to see her, was thrilling and terrifying at the same time. "Thank you. I won't be long." Without waiting for another response, she turned around and rushed back up the stairs.

She spent twenty minutes getting ready.

Fuck. Fuck. Fuck. What were the odds that she'd bump into him here? When Valerie had said Mr. Daniels had been called away to work, she thought it was a lie. She honestly believed he'd left because of her slutty response to his kiss. Well, seeing him here now made her feel much better. Obviously he really was on business and apparently it took him all over the place. Still, the coincidence of him being here at the same place and time as she, was more than a little strange. Considering the mission, she had to be careful.

Jamie decided to stick with something comfortable yet sexy for their nightcap. She stood in front of the mirror after walking into a cloud of perfume, then applied a small amount of makeup and tinted her lips peach. Studying the woman staring back at her didn't settle her nerves at all. She'd always thought that her forehead was too high and her nose too wide, although she had to admit that her lips were full and she had nice green eyes. But her boobs didn't sit where they should, her ass could use some tightening, and she hated the chub on her belly. Knowing that Jack had stared at her while she was braless had been more than a little disturbing. No woman with less-than-perky tits wanted a handsome stranger seeing them hanging there like overripe melons.

She sighed, and turned away from the mirror. *It's just a nightcap, not a marriage proposal.*

For tonight, she chose a pair of black leggings and a loose-fitting purple tunic with slits on the forearms and shoulders, and a pair of sandals. Her only accessories were silver earrings and her favorite silver watch. Simple and chic, but most importantly, comfortable. *And if he hits on you again, the outfit will come off easily....*

As she descended the last set of stairs and walked past the lobby and into the piano bar, Jamie couldn't help thinking about that kiss on the dock less than a week ago. She had almost lost control, and if she were to take a good guess, so did he. The chemistry between them was electric. The way he looked at her as if he wanted to eat her, made her come undone like a spool of thread...on fire.

Jack Daniels was sitting at a private table in the corner with cocktails already waiting. The wind beating against the shutters didn't take away from the romantic ambiance of the room, or of the crisp white linen shirt and dress pants he wore. A heat wave that had nothing to do with the weather in Havana washed over her as Jack stood and pulled a chair out next to him. God, he was handsome. Even more so when he'd trimmed his beard.

Jamie blushed as his smile widened, hinting at that gold tooth again. *What makes a man want a gold tooth?* "You're stunning," he said, his rapt gaze taking her in from toes to eyes. "But I must say, I enjoyed the sight earlier, too."

She chuckled and brushed a few loose strands of hair behind her ear—a nervous habit she'd had since she was eight. "When I was half-dressed and confused?"

His eyes hinted at mischief. "I'll take the half-dressed part any day of the year. But you did seem a little out of it. Everything okay now?"

Jamie sipped the sweet cocktail and nodded. "I'm okay. I must be jetlagged, is all. I only just arrived and already reception is confusing me with someone else." *Yes, perfect answer.* "And you? How was your evening?"

"Boring, actually. But as much as I wasn't thrilled to be called away from that lodge, I'm glad to see you here. I was tempted to leave my number for you before I left."

Fighting another blush, Jamie nodded and took her seat before he realized just how much his presence affected her. "I remember Valerie saying something about your retail business being very lucrative."

He chuckled and took his seat next to her, his thigh only an inch away from hers. "I don't remember telling her what I do for a living."

His sex-inducing scent swirled like a drug through her head. She cleared her throat. "What *do* you do for a living?"

Jack lifted a brow and gave her a sharp glance. "If I told you, my dear, well then I'd—"

"Have to kill me?" Jamie giggled, and took another sip of her cocktail. She was just about to ask where he was staying when a phone rang between them.

After several rings Jack gave her an odd look. "Aren't you going to answer that?"

"Oh, shit." Jamie grabbed her clutch, having forgotten about the cell phone Monty had given her for communication. "Sorry. Excuse me." She got up from her seat and found a quiet spot across the spacious room to answer the call.

"Hello?"

"Did you make it in okay?" Monty asked.

Jamie glanced over at Jack and returned his smile. "Yes. Everything is good, and I even bumped into somebody we know."

His voice hardened. "Who?"

"That sexy guy from the lodge."

"Ah." His gruff tone shifted to one of amusement. "Does he have a big dick?"

"I"—she cleared her throat and forced a straight face as she glanced back at Jack again—"I don't know." She turned her back to her unexpected date and whispered into the phone, "Apparently he got called away from the lodge on business, and now he's here. He called out my name in the lobby and asked me to join him for a nightcap."

Monty chuckled. "Then I suggest you get busy and clear those cobwebs in your panties." There was a short pause before he spoke again. "I don't see why you can't have any fun on your trip, as long as there aren't any hiccups tomorrow. You deserve a good time, twit. I'll let the boss know we're still good for tomorrow."

As much as she wanted to confide in Monty about the mix-up this evening, she decided against it. She didn't want him to worry that something was already amuck, even though she was fairly certain it was only a mistake with reception.

Although receiving the note scared the shit out of her, nothing actually happened from it. Maybe reception confused her with somebody else, or the guy in the suit thought she was another person. After all, her name wasn't listed on the note. Maybe someone was meeting up with the person renting the room before her. Reception had no record of the message and there was no mention of her bringing the briefcase. *Maybe I'm just frazzled. Breathe. Just breathe.* Still, her nerves were frayed over the edge of reason.

"So far so good, Monty." Jamie closed her eyes and breathed deep. "You can count on me." She glanced over her shoulder, eyeing Jack very slowly from dress shoes to eyeballs. God, he looked good. "I might have to listen to your words of wisdom and bring him to my room."

Monty released a sharp bark of laughter. "Good girl. Let me know how it goes. In the meantime, just be careful."

"I will. Talk to you soon." She shut off the phone and slipped it back into her clutch before making her way back to the table.

Jack stood and held her seat as she sat back down. "Sorry about that. Apparently Valerie can't manage without me."

"Ah." Jack took his seat. "I know the feeling. Sometimes it seems like the phone never stops ringing." Jack took a sip of his cocktail, all the while, watching her attentively. "So what makes a woman decide to be a housekeeper? I can't imagine it being a very rewarding job."

Her sudden snort made the corner of his mouth tip up. "It's definitely not rewarding, but I actually like to clean." She shrugged. "I don't really know how to describe it, but…I guess it's kinda like an artist looking at their finished painting. I look at a room and I'm satisfied that I made it look awesome. That sounds pathetic, I know."

Jack shook his head. "Not really. Without housekeepers, hotels and resorts wouldn't exist. We all have a *job* to do." His direct stare made her breath hitch. "Dealing with the people in my profession isn't very rewarding either, especially when deals go south." At Jamie's curt nod, he leaned forward, his gaze intent and packing heat. "Let's talk about something more *rewarding*. What are you looking to do during your stay in Havana?"

You. Jamie leaned back at a safe distance and shrugged. She didn't want him to think her too eager, despite nearly throwing herself on him at the lodge. "I've heard the nightlife is pretty spectacular. That's number one on my to-do list."

"And number two?" His left eyebrow arched.

Jamie couldn't help her nervous laugh. "Check out the sights, I guess."

"That's it? No essential oil massage, or eucalyptus bath? A naked snorkel along the coral reefs midday?"

She raised a brow as her active imagination conjured up strong hands rubbing warm oil all over her back and ass. "No. The most I'll venture into the water is to my ankles." At his bizarre expression, she added, "I've watched too many shark attack documentaries. With my luck, I'd be the next casualty."

"Ah." He leaned back in his chair. "So you're not an adventurer?"

She shook her head. "Not really. I live a pretty lame life."

His gold-toothed grin made her stomach flip over. "Can I ask you a personal question?"

Her cheeks heated. He obviously wasn't a shy man, with all these questions. "Sure."

"Are you single?"

Her hand gripping the glass paused mid lift. Her gaze widened. "Are you?"

"I am."

Jamie cleared her throat and took a deep drink of her cocktail. When she set her glass down, she asked the server loudly, "Can I have a couple shots of Fireball, please?" The waiter looked at her funny. Disappointed, she slunk back in her seat as a heavy heat settled in her stomach. Apparently she would have to deal with Jack and his questions while sober. "Yes, I'm single. Why do you ask?"

Jack leaned forward, his gaze sharp, the meaning in his look unmistakable. "Because I'd like to continue what we started on that dock…unless you've changed your mind?"

Her gaze locked on his. Nothing could make her look away. *Good thing I shaved this morning.* She wanted him. Wanted his hands on her. Craved his lips kissing her lonely flesh as his body connected to hers. But having sex with a stranger was scary, and a little embarrassing. Maybe she wouldn't be good enough, or sexy enough, or maybe she was just unworthy for a one-night stand with a man who could give the most handsome actor in Hollywood a run for his millions.

This time when she waved the waiter over, she asked, "Tequila?" And bless his soul, the young man returned with two shots. Jamie tipped both back, ignoring Jack's amused expression. As the second shot burned an intimate path down her throat and she cringed only slightly, Jack chuckled.

"Did I say something wrong?"

"Uh"—her cheeks flushed again—"No…I just, don't know what to say." *Get a grip of yourself, woman! Grab him by the collar and yank him to your room. Rip his clothes off and fuck the last breath out of him!* "I know we got a little carried away on that dock, and I apologize if I reacted like a slut."

Jack sat back in his chair, his smile devilish. "If you were being a slut, then I guess I was being a whore."

Warm in the stomach, and slightly less embarrassed by his odd compliment, Jamie raised her glass. "Then cheers to us nymphos."

His crooked smile hit her right to the core as Jack polished off the rest of his cocktail. *This is it. Keep it together, woman. You might just get laid tonight.*

"I have an idea." He waggled his eyebrows and Jamie had a sudden vision of that face between her legs. "Let's go dancing." His thumb brushed up and down the side of his empty glass. "I know a place where the dance floor is always packed, the tequila is top of the line, and the music makes you want to move."

God, he made that sound so appealing. "You must be in sales, because you totally sold me on that." Jamie tore her gaze away from the erotic motion of his thumb on that lucky glass and smiled at him. The wind seemed to have settled at just the right time as she took the last sip of her drink.

Jack stood and held out his hand. Before she changed her mind like she did that night on the dock, Jamie set her glass down and slipped her hand in his.

Chapter 5

Sam had to play his cards right, at the same time, he couldn't help his desire for a bit of fun. He knew what he was doing. Nearly twenty years in the business taught him how to deal with a sticky situation. Sink her in deep and hook her hard. Make her feel as if she could trust him, open up to him, and then yank her out of the water.

He had to admit, when Jamie blew into the lobby holding that briefcase and looking frantic, he was disappointed. He wanted her to be one of the good ones. He knew better than to assume the worst right away, but he also knew how to be cautious. It wasn't worth getting too excited over something without enough background information. The fact that she was here with a briefcase could very well be coincidental, but he doubted it. Not when she ran into that lobby as if a dragon blew fire all over the back of her legs. Housekeepers don't travel with briefcases, and they sure as hell don't act as if they'd just broken the law.

But he grinned nonetheless, because he liked her smile. It made the skin at the corner of those stunning green eyes crinkle. She must smile a lot, he imagined.

He kept his focus straight forward, as he vividly recalled staring up at her on those steps without a bra on. Not many men in this world could look away from a set of free-hanging tits. Might as well hang bacon over a dog's mouth.

As he touched the small of her back while they descended the steps and exited the hotel, he wondered if he'd be considered an asshole for taking advantage of her like this. He wanted to fuck her, wanted to make love to her, but at the same time, he wanted to make her pay for trying to blackmail them. He wouldn't let it happen, of course, but still, her plan was set into motion which was why he was here. His job was to get the briefcase and then kill her. Nothing would stop him from fulfilling his duty.

Why did it have to be her? What did they ever do to her? Before the lodge he'd never seen Jamie before, not even in passing. She had the kind of face that was unforgettable.

He thought hard about what he should do with her, as they strolled down the cobblestone streets toward his favorite nightclub. Despite the mini storm that blew in a short while ago, the streets of Havana were right back to their usual nighttime excitement.

The seductive beat of Cuban drums lilted in the air. A cool Caribbean breeze swept through the narrow streets. They passed a man and woman in a heated embrace against the stone façade of a nearby building. Sam's blood raced as the woman's excited sigh met his ears. He wondered if Jamie heard it too and how it made her feel.

His gaze wandered down to the opening of Jamie's shirt at the bare expanse of her smooth shoulder. If he leaned down and kissed her there on that purple flower tattoo, would she sigh in rapture like that woman against the wall?

Jamie glanced up and caught him staring at her shoulder. "How often do you come here on business?"

Sam cleared his throat and looked at her face. There was something about her that made him want to tell her about his life, about his struggles, but he knew better. His solitary life was best kept that way. "Maybe a couple times a year, depending on who calls."

"Must be nice to come here on business," she said in a wistful tone.

Not even close, sweetheart. "It pays the bills."

Around the next corner, the outdoor lights of the nightclub shone like a strobe light. Jamie's surprised gasp and excited expression made him grin. Her honest—or what appeared to be honest—reaction to sights and sounds appealed to him. A thought struck his mind that only a person who'd never really traveled would react in such a way. Which made him wonder how worldly this woman really was. If her intention was to blackmail them for ten million, wouldn't she be more sly and seductive—not sweet and chatty?

People were dancing in the street right outside of the club. Hips grinded, lips touched. Women danced together. Men danced together. This place was a whole world of its own. A man and a woman could be anybody here.

"Here we are." He guided Jamie toward the wide-open doors and into the packed nightclub. "What do you think?" He shouted through the music.

Her smile was all the answer he needed, especially when he noticed her hips moving to the beat already. She closed her eyes and swayed to the tune, lifted her arms above her head and let the music take her away. Sam took the opportunity to admire her body, how her full breasts stretched the purple shirt to its max, how her curvy hips moved in sweet seduction.

Hypnotized, he stepped closer, into her body's curve and began moving along with her to the bump and grind of the music, a sway that could only belong to the rhythmic heat that was Cuban. Everywhere he looked, women were half-dressed. Men drooled and ass grinded against any broad that would accept their attention. Sweat mingled and trickled with perfume and cologne, while eyes appreciated and bodies loved with abandon.

Sam slipped an arm around her waist and drew her closer. When she opened her eyes in that lazy, *take me, I don't mind*, kind of way, he knew what was on the menu tonight. Jamie let her arms rest around his shoulders, and when he leaned down and put his mouth on hers, she responded exactly as he remembered from that night on the dock.

Passion. Electricity. Full-body heat.

As her sweet lips mingled with his and her hips pressed harder, more urgently against him, Sam didn't want to be in this place anymore. He wanted to take her back to his room and show her how pleasing the Caribbean breeze felt against naked, sweaty flesh.

He leaned closer and murmured in her ear as they swayed smoothly to the music. "Can I tell you something?"

She looked up and gave a shy nod. His blood simmered by that sexy expression.

"I've thought about that kiss on the dock since I left Sharp Ridge."

Her sweet lips tipped up in a half smile. "Me too."

He gave her a wolfish glance. "Whatever happens here is your decision to make. We can go to your room and find out just how hot this thing is between us, or we can get drunk on tequila and go our separate ways. Whatever you want."

She was just about to answer but stopped short when a movement behind her caught Sam's eye. Without expressing the sudden anger welling up, Sam nodded to the man whose face was well known to him. The fact that he was here could mean only one thing.

Without startling her, Sam leaned closer, his eyes still trained on the person standing twenty paces behind her back. "I'll be right back. Don't go anywhere."

She nodded, oblivious to his sudden change in demeanor, or to the fact that the years of training and survival mode had rushed back to the surface, pushing away any and all thoughts of the previous hour spent with her.

He left her on the dancefloor and followed the man who had disappeared into the dark hallway leading to the washrooms. A thought crossed his mind that she had arranged this, but Jamie had no idea beforehand that Sam would take her to a nightclub. Unless Norman the Norwegian was paid to follow her and keep her safe at all costs. She could afford to pay him with the ten million McCoy was dishing out for her silence.

Whatever the case, the blond monster would be hard to take down, having at least a hundred pounds over Sam, and all of it muscle.

Prepared to fight, he slipped the small but deadly titanium knife from the pocket of his slacks and held it hidden in the palm of one hand, as he pushed the bathroom door open with the other. The door swung shut behind him, muffling the music. An old florescent light flickered above the sinks, making the funky bright orange and blue walls hard to decipher where the walls started or ended. He jerked, surprised and a little disoriented from the lighting as two men exited the same stall.

The second the main door swung shut behind them, the stall door beside him burst open smashing against the frame. Before Sam could react, he was hit from the side and violently shoved into the counter against the opposite wall. He grunted at the biting pain as his hip collided hard against the cement vanity. Sam sucked in a sharp breath and squinted hard, trying to block out the throbbing ache. Norman came at him again and again, bruising his ribs with his deadly knuckles.

Sam grit his teeth and flipped the knife in his hand, swinging it out with all of his strength, slicing through the air but missing his target. Norman released a deep guttural laugh as his massive fist pounded into Sam's ribs, making him stumble back a few feet. He struggled to breathe, fought to maintain his footing as a wave of heat threatened to take him down. He managed to block a hit to the face, but couldn't catch his breath fast enough to give one of his own. Maybe this was it. Maybe his days were finally over, Sam thought, as the brawny Norwegian rushed him again.

But he couldn't die now. He was too stubborn for that, and his brothers were counting on him to see this job through—no matter the cost.

As Norman came at him full force, Sam used the advantage of his smaller size and speed to squat down at the last second, as Norman swung at his head with all of his weight. Sam curved the knife up, jabbing the blade deep into his opponent's stomach He pushed against Norman's shoulder, shoving him down to twist the knife up to his heart with all of the strength and force he had left.

Norman's groan echoed through the washroom as he sunk to his knees then fell forward. Dark blood oozed onto the tiled floor as Sam pulled his knife out of Norman's flesh. He moved to the sink and stared at his reflection for a long while, even knowing he could be seen, as he absently rinsed the blood from the blade. His face appeared gaunt and tired. His eyes held no emotion other than acceptance of his life and his path. *Sam Hayes, you might as well be a fucking doll.* A powerful surge of bile rushed up his throat from what he'd just done, and what he'd become after all these years. He shook it off, and cursed himself for letting his emotions nearly make him puke. *Shrug it off. It's just another hit.*

He walked away from the mirror, and the man staring back at him. Sometimes he didn't care if he got caught, but for his brothers and their families, he couldn't stay there and risk being seen.

As the last breath gurgled out of Norman the Norwegian's mouth, Sam slipped the knife back into his pocket and exited the washroom. He swept through the crowd, thankful that nobody had seen him and returned to Jamie who was now standing at a high table chatting with a man. Sam gave him a sharp glare and the guy disappeared into the crowd. Jamie seemed shocked by the guy's sudden departure, but Sam didn't care. She seemed to shy away as he walked up, but said nothing.

His side ached so bad he was certain he'd cracked something, but he couldn't let her see his pain. She needed to believe that he was just some random businessman here on a boring job, whether he looked like hell or not.

With the vivid image of Norman lying in the bathroom, and the beautiful face of Jamie in front of him, Sam decided that he needed something soft, something to take the pain away of what he'd just done. He took her hand and led her back to the dancefloor.

As everyone else swung about, gyrating against each other to the fast, hip-swinging music, Sam held Jamie close and guided her in a slow rhythm with him. He breathed in the flowery scent of her hair as she put her cheek to his chest and followed his lead. The lights and chaos and laughter in the club didn't exist as he swept his hand around the curve of her hip and up her back to the nape of her neck.

Jamie pulled back and looked up at him with awareness, her seductive eyes pulling him in like a fish in a net. He leaned down as she pushed up, and when their lips met on that crowded dance floor, he knew he would have her tonight.

His heart pounded with excitement, and his cock ached to be inside her as their lips mingled and their tongues tasted. He wanted to own her and punish her at the same time.

Without a word, he took her hand and led her out the door. As they headed back to the hotel along the narrow street, he found a secluded spot and pressed her against the stone wall. She didn't say a word, didn't pull away from him as he braced his hands on each side of her head and leaned down to capture her lips for another kiss. Her whimper of pleasure made his blood dance like that packed nightclub.

The sensual beat of the Cuban drums in the background matched the pounding of his heart as he moved his hands away from the wall to cup her breasts. They were full and heavy, as he imagined they would be when he saw her without a bra. God, that was such a turn on. He'd wanted to ravage her right there on those stairs in her flustered and nervous state. He could've taken the briefcase then and there as well, but he didn't. He wanted to know about her. Needed to know what she was all about.

"I want you," he murmured.

Jamie's back hugged the wall as her arms snaked around his neck. "*Yes.*"

He moved down and kissed her breasts through her shirt and bra, instigating a throaty moan from her perfect lips. Then he trailed his hand down and cupped the apex of her trembling thighs, feeling the hot wetness there right through her pants. That was all the encouragement he needed.

He took her hand again and led her back to the hotel, his steps quick and sure. As he led her up the stairs into the hotel and to his room, he knew what he needed.

Sam wanted to forget what just happened in that bathroom. What he needed was her softness, her smile, and her body beneath his. Right now he didn't care who she was or what she was about. He'd cross that path when it came.

He shut the door to his suite and switched on a lamp as she walked ahead of him, taking in the details of the space, her sandals clicking softly on the wooden floor. A large, queen-sized bed dominated the cozy room flanked by two small bedside tables. Being a man, he didn't much care about the décor—everything was a different shade of brown—but she seemed impressed. None of that mattered when all he wanted was to toss her onto that bed and have his way with her.

Jamie moved to the narrow double doors leading to his balcony. "Can I open them?"

When she glanced over her shoulder, he nodded. "Whatever you want."

She smiled and turned around, opened the old wooden doors. Havana Port twinkled a short distance away. A sliver of a moon highlighted rooftop terraces. A gust of wind billowed the curtains, but his gaze was caught in the sway of her golden hair.

"It's beautiful."

As if in a trance, he walked up behind her, slid her hair to the side and kissed the back of her neck. Jamie released a deep sigh and turned around to face him. The knowing look in her eyes was the key to his fulfillment.

With the balcony doors to his room wide open, he slid her shirt up and over her body, his rapt gaze followed her golden hair as it fell back over her shoulders. He swept her hair to the side again, leaned down and kissed her tattooed shoulder as he wanted to an hour before. Her head fell back as he kissed and licked her soft flesh, working his way down to her breasts. Jamie let her head fall back and expelled a throaty moan as she reached back and unhooked her bra, pulling away the offending garment and tossing it on the floor. He sucked her nipples hard, desperate with anger and resentment at his life, yet thrilled to be here, in his room, with her. She moaned soft and deep, more seductive than the woman shrouded by darkness in the street.

They didn't say a word. Only touched. Breathed in the scent of their arousal. Listened to the hushed moans and sighs of pleasure.

Jamie unbuttoned his shirt as Sam hooked his fingers in her leggings and rolled them down the exquisite length of her shapely legs. He took his time, showing her how much she turned him on. He knelt down with the descent of her leggings, kissing and licking her tender flesh. As she stepped out of them, he kissed her hot pussy through the soaked material of her panties. But as Sam tongued her panties and lifted his hands to remove them, Jamie stepped back and shook her head, eyes dark with desire and mystery. With a coy smile she retreated to his bed and sat on the edge, clad in nothing but tanned skin and lacy black panties.

What a beautiful sight.

A rumble of animalistic desire growled under his breath as she crooked her finger for him to come to her. And come to her, he did. He approached cautiously, suddenly worried she had a nasty trick up her sleeve, just when his work instincts were put on hold and his dick was harder than the coral reef out there.

But when he stepped between her open thighs at the edge of the bed, Jamie stared up at him with luminous eyes and reached up to peel away his unbuttoned shirt. It slipped off to pool on the floor behind his feet. Fucking hell, the way she touched him so softly, yet with an expert touch, made him want to shove her down and fuck her hard. But he had to control the animal within.

Next, her fingernail touched the top of his chest and scraped an erotic path all the way down to his navel, twirling around the dark path of hair leading to excitement. He grit his teeth. She unhooked his slacks and unzipped him with the finesse of a woman who knew what she wanted, and wanted it now.

Sam sucked in a sharp breath as Jamie boldly reached into his boxers and pulled out his achingly stiff rod. *Yes.*

"Mmm," she moaned, and glanced up at him with hungry eyes before she leaned close and flicked her hot tongue over his head.

Sam grit his teeth as he watched her work him like a horny woman on a mission. *Jesus Christ.* He blew out a long breath as she licked around his head and then under the base of his shaft, before she took him as far into her mouth as she could handle. He closed his eyes in pleasure as her throat cinched around him and she forced herself to take more, right to the back of her throat.

This wasn't good. He should be the one in control, not the one being handled like a young man about to chuck it almost instantly. Her hot, wet, suctioning mouth captivated him.

He released a deep moan and feathered his fingers through her soft hair. As if of their own will, his hips rocked forward. But before he lost control, he gripped her hair, gently pulled her head back and brought his lips to hers. He kissed her hard, showing her through actions how much she turned him on, how much her attention pleased him. Then he cupped her shoulders and laid her back on the bed. It was time to turn up the music.

Like a content feline, Jamie lounged over the plush blankets, her hot gaze trained on him as Sam yanked down his pants and boxers. Her mouth opened seductively, and her soft moan of pleasure as she stared at his nakedness turned him on even more.

He was fueled by much more than her passion. He had the weight of the world on his shoulders, and she was about to be his target of release. Hurting her wasn't an option, pleasing her was his mission.

Sam sprawled out over her body, kissing and licking every inch of her quivering skin. As he worked his way down her soft, warm flesh, her hips began to writhe beneath him, clearly eager for more. He gripped her panties and slid them off with reckless speed, before he crouched between her legs and kissed her pussy with the dual thrill of his tongue.

"*Oh….*" Her beautiful lips parted for a deep, lingering sigh.

Jamie gripped the bedding and shrieked as he licked and nipped and blew on her sensitive clit, all the while his hands pressing her knees to the bed, spreading her wide and open for him. Now he was in control. She was about to become his possession.

He delved his tongue from the tip of her clit right down to the dark treasure of her ass. She cried out and squirmed, her hips lifting off the mattress. As he licked back up to the trembling crest of her wet lips, and flicked his tongue hard on her clit over and over again, Jamie released a throaty moan and her body stilled.

She came hard, her whole body quaking in ecstasy, her cries throaty and passionate. He enjoyed every second of it.

As she lay there panting and flushed a moment later, Sam reached over to the nightstand for the packet of condoms he was glad he bought on a whim, and quickly slipped one on. Her body was still quivering as he nudged his painfully hard head against her clit and rubbed there softly, up and down and around, driving her wild.

She jerked hard with every push he gave. Shuddered each time he ground his hips against her. She was wet and glistening and ready to take him. Sam gripped his shaft, gently probing with only the tip, feeding a little more and a little more with each teasing thrust.

"Yes," she whimpered, rocking against him, wanting him deeper, and urging him to push harder. It triggered the hungry beast waiting to be unleashed.

He gave her exactly that, pushing in deep, making her suck in a sharp gasp of surprise. He stared into her wide eyes, thrilled by her reaction. Fueled to give her so much more. God, she was tight.

He shouldn't be doing this. Shouldn't be having sex with a woman who was after his family for money. But he couldn't help himself. Couldn't stop the need to bury himself deep inside her, lose himself inside her hot, wet heat and forget about all the bad shit that'd happened in his life. This was the only way to find release for a tormented man like him.

Curving over her body, he was entranced how her tight nipples brushed against his chest. Her hips ground against his, meeting every hard thrust with her own rough need. She sighed and whimpered and moaned and it was the best music a man could hear. Jamie tightened around him, her impending climax gripping him hard, and before he could get a grip of himself and hold on just a little bit longer, he felt his own rush draw to the surface.

Her eyes widened and her body shuddered. She cried out and gripped his hips, digging into his flesh with her fingernails. *Yes, feel it.* Sam pushed faster, cupping her bum to lift her higher, gratified by her fluttering walls gripping him so tight. A deep, guttural moan escaped his lips as he stilled and released his torment, coming right along with her. He thought his dick would explode he came so hard. He squinted tight and blew out a sharp breath. Never before had he felt such a rush, such animal passion with a woman. He wanted to rip off that condom, feel her nakedness, and come deep inside her.

As Sam rolled off her body, his breath short and sharp, he didn't know if he should feel regret or relief. They lay there side-by-side, both staring up at the ceiling, neither saying a word.

After a long stretch of silence which became more awkward by the minute, Jamie pushed up to sit at the edge of the bed, and glanced down at him over her shoulder. Her cheeks flushed and she looked away from him. "Maybe I should head back to my room…."

That wasn't what he wanted to hear. "Why can't you stay? Did I do something wrong?" *God, you idiot. Now she'll think you want more than a casual fuck.* But maybe he did. This whole situation was unlike anything he'd experienced before. He could have her for a few more days yet. Really give it to her good before duty called.

"Uh, do you want me to stay?" A slow, almost unsure smile touched her rosy lips as she glanced back at him. That shy smile made him want to take her again, and again, until he had nothing left to give.

"Maybe I do. Would you like to stay the night? I promise I'm pretty good at cuddling." *And getting hard again.*

She giggled and shook her head in obvious incredulity. "I've only been here for two days—"

"And the problem is?" *Careful, Sam…careful.*

She shrugged and her cheeks took on a healthy glow again. He liked how she looked when she blushed. He wanted her ass to glow like that from his palm print. There were so many things he could do to her. This was just the beginning. "I'm here for a few more days."

Sam pushed up and kissed her shoulder, smiling to himself as her nipple tightened. "Well then, what harm would one night away from your room do?" *Everything, you fool.*

She thought about it for a short moment, then looked him directly in the eyes. "Okay. I'll stay. But just for tonight."

Sam couldn't help his impish grin, despite his mind screaming that this wasn't a good idea. He pulled her back down on the bed with him and wrapped her up in his arms. Although he was lying when he said he was good at cuddling, having her nestled up to him felt good, like a high school kid acing a test, or something like that.

At first he thought it was ridiculous how Gabe and Terry's life had changed when the right woman stepped in, but now he wasn't so sure. They looked happy, relieved, as if the chaos of the business no longer existed. If only that were true for Sam. He didn't only work for McCoy—he also contracted on the side. Now that Terry had left the drug world, with Gabe right behind him, Sam still had to earn an income on his own. He was well known in the underworld and a week wouldn't go by without a call for another job. A busy man didn't have time to settle down, but he often thought what settling with a good woman would be like.

Sometime during the night, Sam woke up with a painful erection against her back. He swept the palm of his hand over the soft curve of her rib cage to her waist and over her hip. He kissed the back of her shoulder as he gently nudged his cock between her ass cheeks. Jamie stirred, released a soft moan, and opened her legs. Sam smiled against her back, more turned on than ever over her desire for more. As he slid a condom on for the second time that night and slid his cock between her glorious lips, already wet and ready for him, he considered himself a lucky man.

He fucked her like that, from behind, with one thigh propped over his legs, her head back against the pillow as she cried out in the balmy night.

They fell asleep like that, wrapped together, wet, and satisfied. Two hours later, Sam woke up to find her gone, and he realized that he was an idiot. He knew he shouldn't have slept with her, but he couldn't help himself. And now, she could be anywhere, plotting against him, knowing his weakness for her.

Angry with himself for thinking with the wrong head, he whipped out of bed and checked his belongings, cursing aloud at his stupidity. Nothing looked out of the ordinary, but he was still suspicious that she may have gone through his things and learned his true identity. He couldn't even remember sleeping so soundly in a very long time, and of course it had to be now…on a dangerous mission…with her.

Once he was sure his belongings were secure, he grabbed his cell and phoned Gabe, who answered on the second ring despite the crude hour. "What do you want?"

Sam inhaled and exhaled a few breaths, not really sure why he called Gabe. What if he told his brother his suspicions and then Gabe went after her? *What if I'm wrong about her?* He lowered his head, not really looking at anything in particular, and tried to come up with something random. "I was just wondering if your room was comfortable." He closed his eyes and shook his head the second those words came out.

Gabe groaned into the phone. "Really? At 4:37 a.m. you're concerned for my well-being?"

Sam grit his teeth. "Yes." *Why the fuck did I call him?*

"What did you do?" Gabe's gruff, tired voice made Sam realize that he should say something. He knew that if he didn't, and something happened, Gabe would have that over his head for the rest of Sam's pathetic life. Plus, Gabe flew all the way over here to assist him on this mission.

He sat there, shoulders slumped, slouching as if the air itself was fighting against him. "I think it's her."

"Who?"

He opened his eyes and glared at the wall as if Gabe could see. "The housekeeper, you idiot. Who else have I been watching?"

Gabe yawned into the phone. "You never know with you. Are you sure it's her?"

Sam released a sharp breath. "Yes."

There was a long pause before Gabe chuckled. "You fucked her, didn't you? Once again you let your dick make the decisions. You should know better."

Sam growled into the phone. "You think I don't know that? I set her up last night with a note to her room. She came into the lobby with the briefcase. Long story short, she was gone when I woke up this morning."

"You're sure she didn't leave because you talk too much?"

"Fuck off," he said, but couldn't help a sudden bark of laughter—not from Gabe's teasing, but from this fucked-up situation he'd put himself in. He could've grabbed that briefcase as she stood on the stairs, and ran off with it—just like that. But no. Like a horny fool, he had to take her out for drinks and then plow her.

"Well, did she say anything to confirm she's who you think she is?"

"Not really, but she acts too nervous and sketchy to be a woman on vacation."

Gabe chuckled. "I believe you, bud. Just try to stay calm and be smart. Once this is over tomorrow, you'll have a new life ahead of you."

A new life. Yeah, right. "Another thing. I bumped into Norman last night."

It took a moment for Gabe to respond. "The Norwegian? I thought you two were sort of friends."

"Yeah. We were." The look in Norman's eyes while he died was still too fresh in Sam's mind. "He left me no choice, Gabe. I didn't want to do it." His eyes widened as it struck him deep and hard that he didn't want to kill Jamie either.

"I know." Gabe sighed hard into the phone. "You think he was working for her?"

His chest tightened and suddenly it was tough to breathe. Gabe had no idea of the war raging in his mind over this situation with Jamie. If it hurt him to kill Norman, how painful would it be to end Jamie's life?

Sam shook his head. *Focus.* "Why else would he come after me?" he belted into the phone. "She must've offered a big payout to him to go back on his word to me." He exhaled deep, trying to forget how easy his knife went through the Norwegian's guts. He didn't want to do it. He and Norman went way back, and the big guy had even saved his life once. But it was either Norman or himself, and any man would fight to stay alive. Still, this was the first time he regretted his job. The very first time he wanted to take it all back. He grit his teeth and tried to focus on the task at hand, namely the woman who managed to trick him. "Just be ready for tomorrow so we can go home and forget about this shit."

"Okay, bud. Calm down. Are you sure you'll be able to go through with it?"

Sam pictured the look of ecstasy on her face as he moved inside her body. He grit his teeth, knowing all too well the sound of her sighs, the heated look in her eyes. "When have I not?" He hung up the phone before Gabe could say anything else to piss him off.

He pulled the metal briefcase from beneath the bed, punched in his code, and opened the lid. Sam stared down at his trusty 9mm Sig Sauer cradled by velvet inserts, and wondered if he could really do it. He'd never slept with a woman he was supposed to kill before. The fact that she managed to break a few bricks from his wall without even doing anything bothered him most.

Today he'd follow her, maybe even find a way to confront her without making her suspicious. Either way, he needed to reassure himself that no matter what, he had to pull the trigger.

Chapter 6

Day three of the mission, Jamie had woken up and snuck out of bed to dress as quickly as she could without waking Jack. She couldn't believe she had actually went to his room and had sex with him on her second night in Havana. Yes, she had wanted him back at the lodge, but to bump into him here, on her so-called vacation, was both perfect and inconvenient at the same time.

Still aglow, yet embarrassed how easily she had given in when he took her hand and led her away from the nightclub, Jamie stared at his sleeping form and smiled. He looked so carefree and handsome, lying there, softly snoring. What a night they had. Of all the relationships she'd had over the years, none of those men compared to the explosive connection she had with this man, this stranger.

On impulse, she crept closer, leaned down, and kissed his cheek, ran her fingers through his thick, curly hair. Maybe it was meant as a good-bye, or maybe she just wanted to give him a small gesture of affection. She'd made a few mistakes in the past. Used her body to pay for the drugs she thought she desperately needed. But that was a long time ago, and she didn't recognize that woman any more. The woman in her skin today would never sleep with a stranger—ever—not even for a pile of money. She wasn't the kind of woman out looking for a good time. There was a mission to see through, and another twenty-five grand to make.

Now that her bills were paid, she didn't really need the final payment. She could take off, leave the briefcase, and never look back. But Jamie was never one to take the easy way out. Life had dealt her a tough blow before. It wouldn't take her down this time either. She deserved the rest of the money. Once this mission was complete, for once in her life she wanted to be carefree, even if only for a short while.

Last night with Jack had meant something to her, and that thought was scary to say the least. She didn't even know him any more than the man who carried her suitcase up to her room.

He stirred and rolled over, turning his back to her. It was then that she noticed several scars on his back. Her eyes widened. She reached out and gently touched what looked like a perfect small circle just below his right shoulder blade. What would make a scar like that, she wondered. A bullet? Her heartbeat quickened as her stunned gaze moved to the next scar just beneath the other, a long thin line that could be a cut from a surgeon's knife, or a blade of a different kind.

Troubled by the sight and unsure what to think, Jamie pulled the coverlet up and covered his naked torso. She had much to think about on this crazy journey. Seeing those scars that didn't seem to fit the description of a man in retail, made her wonder who he really was. Yet at the same time, she knew well that everyone in this world had a past, whether it was good or not. That didn't make the person who they were today.

Jamie sat there for a long while, watching him sleep, secretly hoping that he wouldn't judge her as she refused to judge him. With a sad smile, she stood, and snuck out of his room.

As she headed back to her room, up the stairs to the next floor, and down the dismal and narrow hallway, a bald man sitting at a group of high-back chairs looked up from his newspaper and smirked. Jamie looked away from his intent stare and blushed, knowing she must look like a train wreck on her walk of shame.

Best thing for her to do would be to set aside the events of last night and try to enjoy the rest of the day without thinking how it felt being in Jack's arms. After her shower, she decided to go for a nice walk and check out the sights. She had nine hours to kill before the meeting.

Up until a few days ago, her life prospects were shady at best. She never imagined ever being able to come here to this beautiful place, even if it was on a mission that could be considered dangerous. Just knowing she had caught up on her bills, and had plenty of money left, made her feel on top of the world.

The day before her flight to Cuba, Jamie had strolled into Jones's club after receiving her first payment from Monty. Her entire body shook and it felt like a wrench squeezed around her heart, but she still paid her dues as she promised she would.

Jones looked up from his notorious red sheathed accounting book that day, with a sly smile. "You look like you could use a hit." He withdrew a thin slab of polished jade, with a three-inch-high mound of cocaine sitting on top—a fake promise of paradise to many victims. "How about a big bump for old time's sake, eh, babe? I'll carve out a line for you...."

Jamie stared at the cream-colored personal stash that was uncut. She exhaled, feeling the wrench around her heart release as she shook her head. "I don't need that in my life anymore," she said with stark conviction, and tossed the envelope onto his desk. As she headed back to the door leading into the main area of the club, his two bouncers stepped forward, blocking her exit. Jamie lifted her chin and faced them head-on, knowing that if they were ordered, they could hurt her, or worse. Never again would she let herself be treated like a lapdog without a good fight.

"Let her go," Jones said. "She'll be back. She always comes back."

Never. I'll take a bullet before I bow to you or that shit again.

Immediately after leaving the club, Jamie cleared up what she owed to the landlord and other outstanding debts. Within three days she'd gone from not knowing how she was going to survive, to having almost twenty thousand in her pocket. Now, she was in Cuba, enjoying the wild tropical nights, the beaches, and the culture—a far cry from life at home. While she was amazed at the drastic change in scenery, the weather, and the attention from Jack, she still had a mission to complete.

The first meeting would take place this evening.

Monty promised that all would run smoothly as long as she followed the instructions exactly. All she had to do was make an exchange and then wait for a phone call to make the second delivery at another destination. Although she was scared half to death about what she was doing, she knew she had to go through with it.

Not so long ago she was a tough cookie who sold blow with the best of them. Not her most shining moment, but it was a part of her past, and she was just a dumb kid trying to make a few bucks. Then she had managed to really screw up her life by getting into the drugs she was supposed to sell. Life had a funny way of making good people suffer. Her life in particular had been a constant whirlwind of mistakes. But she cleaned up her act and she was proud of herself for that. Now, with this job ahead of her, she had to bring up that tough character and get through this in one piece. Monty was counting on her, and Jamie wasn't going to let him down. She couldn't bear to lose Monty's trust and friendship because she'd made a mistake. Jamie had nobody else. He was her only family, and if he was getting money out of this deal as well, then she couldn't afford to fail.

Along the beautiful cobblestone streets she was in awe by the incredible architecture of the buildings. Some places were getting a fresh coat of bright-colored paint while others seemed to be in a decrepit state. Many buildings were in the midst of renovation, keeping with the historical charm of the city. Laundry hung out of windows. Vined plants connected from building to building. Some of the streets were so narrow she couldn't believe cars drove on them. The cars themselves were from the fifties and sixties, and in every color imaginable. So much color and vitality surrounded her at every corner.

Laughter and music filled the air. A balmy wind swept through the streets, kicking up dust along its path. A man on a motorbike with wicker baskets piled higher than his head, whizzed past at an alarming speed. Jamie whirled around and watched in shock as he veered around traffic and didn't drop a single basket. Kids ran unsupervised every which way, and adults could be seen walking around with open liquor, even gambling in the streets. So much to see in this busy place. So much to take in.

"Taxi?"

Jamie spun around with a start as a young man on a bicycle taxi pulled up beside her. He hopped off the bike and gestured to the seat behind him. Jamie stared in disbelief at the passenger seat which looked like a chair that might've come from his kitchen. She wasn't certain if the chair had been screwed to the wooden board beneath it, or if it just sat there freely. Either way, the contraption looked precarious at best.

"No, thank you." She turned away and kept walking.

Five seconds later someone touched her arm. She glanced down to find a young girl in a tattered blue dress smiling up at her.

"Where you come from?"

"Canada. Do you live here?"

"Oh yes." The little girl smiled wide, revealing a mouth with several missing teeth. "Up there." She pointed up to one of the ramshackle buildings and Jamie's heart sank. The girl reached into the pocket of her skirt and withdrew a single cigar, gesturing for Jamie to buy it.

Jamie stared down at the little girl's dirty fingers and blinked hard. She didn't know what to say to the girl. Maybe she had to beg for her food, or dig in the garbage for a morsel. Feeling sympathetic for the girl who was obviously poor, Jamie reached into her clutch and was about to give her a few dollars for the cigar when she sensed someone behind her. A spicy vanilla aroma assaulted her senses. Her pulse raced immediately and a familiar ache blazed between her legs. Apparently getting her wits together wasn't going to happen, not with him around.

"I wouldn't do that if I were you. You'll have every kid within a mile trying to sell you something worth less than what you pay."

She couldn't get enough of that smooth, deep voice.

Jamie turned around and smiled up at the handsome face she had kissed only a short while ago, as she left him lying there naked. "Good morning." She remembered every vivid detail from last night, but as much as she enjoyed being with him, Jamie was also scared to stick around. If she stayed until the morning with him, then she ran the risk of starting something she shouldn't. Best to be aloof with a man who was still a stranger. "I'm sorry I took off like that." Her cheeks heated and she cleared her throat. The little girl was still standing there watching and listening. "I'm not used to...staying."

She wanted to run her fingers through his hair again. Wanted to touch his scars and learn where they came from. Most of all she wanted him to kiss her over and over as he pushed deep inside her body.

She took a calming breath and squared her shoulders, faced him straight on and tried not to appear like she was thinking about having him in *her* room this time.

"I'm free for part of the afternoon." He reached out and ruffled the young girl's hair. "Run along now." The girl stuck out her tongue and took off down the street.

Jamie stared after her, flustered by Jack's presence, and confused about his exchange with the girl. "Do you know her?"

"I've seen her around many times. She's a *jintero*. A street hustler."

Jamie's eyes widened as she watched the girl run up to another person and do the same thing. "I never would've guessed that sweet little thing to be a hustler."

Jack chuckled. "They're everywhere. She's harmless enough. There are many poor people in this city, especially in the Old Town. Some of them have learned several languages in order to sell to the tourists. People aren't always what they appear to be, right?"

Jamie fought to control the shock jolting through her by his last words. Did he know something about why she was here? "I suppose you're right," she said, as calmly as possible. "I never really thought about it."

He stared hard at her for a moment, before he gestured to the street ahead. "Care to walk with me?"

Jack seemed to know where he was going, and she had no solid plans until tonight. "Sure. I'd like that." At least he'd make sure she didn't get ripped off by a child.

As they walked down the narrow street, music filled the air from the open bars as well as the street musicians. Jamie tried not to keep staring up at Jack as they walked side-by-side at a slow pace. She had no idea what to say to him. Maybe she should apologize for her behavior last night. The grim line of his mouth and the intent focus of his gaze worried her. He seemed pissed-off.

"Look, about last night. I'm really embarrassed—"

"About taking off, or about what happened?" He glanced down at her, almost with accusation in his eyes. Her chest tightened, unsure if he was really upset that she'd left him, or perhaps he believed she really was a slut after all and routinely fucked strange men. "I admit I was disappointed to find you gone when I woke up. I've never known a woman to do that before."

He slowed to a stop and faced her. His thorough perusal made Jamie suddenly very conscious about her appearance, even though he'd already seen her naked. He knew the feel of her body, the sound of her moans. He knew all those torrid details. Why did she have the impression that he was judging her?

She swallowed hard. "I'm sorry. I...I just, felt that I should return back to my room, is all. I hope I didn't upset you?" He shrugged, but the expression on his face and in his eyes seemed as if he didn't believe her.

Jamie reached out and touched his arm, only to pull back when he stared down at her hand as if she'd burned him. Maybe he resented her for what happened between them last night, or maybe she really was an asshole for leaving. But she couldn't help her feelings and emotions. She couldn't take it all back and wake up in his arms this morning. How could she make him understand that she was scared? The clean Jamie Fields had always been scared, and never let a man get too close. Without even knowing, Jack Daniels had found a crack in the wall erected around her, and managed to dig his fingers between those solid bricks.

"I've never done this before, Jack. Really. I wanted to stay with you, but I didn't know if I should. That's all. I swear."

He nodded and continued walking. Confused, Jamie followed him and nearly had to run to keep up, his strides were too long for her short legs. "Did I do something wrong?"

He shook his head, almost as if he was in self-doubt. "No. I just had a bad phone call this morning. That's not your fault." He offered a quick smile. "Care for a drink? I know I could use one."

She checked her watch and laughed out loud. "It's 10 a.m."

He seemed to struggle keeping his expression straight. "Look around you. Does it look like it matters to them?"

A group of men were laughing across the street, each of them passing around a large brown bottle. They didn't seem to notice the world around them. Maybe Havana didn't fall under the usual customs many other people lived by.

"Okay. Drink it is," she said, a little more at ease. She was on vacation after all. Why not let loose and enjoy herself? She needed to get her mind off the mission at least for a few hours. All she could think about was that the exchange could possibly end her life, or at the very least, get her into some serious trouble. After what happened with Jones, she didn't need any more problems in her life.

They fell in step again at a more leisure pace. Cars honked around them, people laughed and shouted in the streets. Everywhere she looked, people were smiling. Everywhere something exciting was happening. But she suddenly didn't want this. The idea of bringing him back to her room had a much more satisfying appeal, even if he did seem upset by something. She couldn't stop thinking about his hands on her, even as her mind fought to control her fears of the meeting tonight.

"So you didn't get to tell me why you're not at the lodge," he added.

Unsure how to answer that without sounding suspicious, she decided on a half-truth. "Well, a friend offered me a trip." She shrugged. "I couldn't refuse such a beautiful place as this. It's like a whole other world here."

"That it is. Havana is a place where lovers meet and transactions are made."

Jamie frowned. *And transactions are made.* Odd that he would say that when that's exactly what she was about to do in a few hours. "Is that what you're here for?"

He faced her now, a dark, almost questioning expression on his face. "My work always involves transactions. How about you?"

She raised a brow, confused by his strange behavior. "I'm on vacation. I think we both know my job involves cleaning up after people, not making transactions." *Please let that be a good enough answer.*

He shrugged. "Fair enough."

"Must be nice to travel to places like this and deal with people."

When he didn't answer, Jamie decided that maybe his job wasn't really all that great. Perhaps she should just leave it at that. Even though it was nice to at least know somebody so far from home, and they'd already spent a night together, his vague response to his work bothered her. Was he hiding something as she hid something from him?

Jamie opened her mouth to ask more about his work when he halted. "This is my favorite spot. Right here." He guided her to a narrow door that looked nothing like the entrance to a decent bar. When she stepped inside, an idea sprung to mind that this place could host a murder scene. Any questions she'd had about his work seemed inappropriate for the moment.

The bar was tiny and in desperate need of renovation. Three shabby tables were lined up on one side, with dilapidated chairs leaning against them. On the other side was a row of booths, the leather seats worse for wear. Two drunk men sat at one end of the small bar, situated in the middle of the room, arguing in Spanish. They didn't seem to notice as Jack led Jamie to one of the roughshod booths. A lone man sat on the other side of the bar. He didn't look up at all when they walked in.

Jamie sat carefully, hoping the cracked leather on the seat didn't rip the new dress she had just purchased. She glanced around and grimaced as she noticed nicotine or something much worse running down the walls from ceiling to floor. The wood floors also could use a good scrubbing to her housekeeping eye. This was where Jack wanted to take her? Not exactly romantic.

She took in the atmosphere with suppressed disgust as Jack took his seat across from her.

"I know it's not the best looking place, but nobody makes a mojito like Zamira. She has a secret ingredient that nobody will ever discover."

"You must know a lot of people around here."

He nodded. "I've been coming to Havana for almost ten years now. One of the drunks over there is her husband, Luis."

"And the guy over there?"

Jack glanced over his shoulder and shrugged. "No idea."

The fact that he took her to a place where he knew some people was encouraging, even though she worried she'd return home with a disease. Still, he seemed happy to be in this tiny, ramshackle bar, and she was glad for some familiar company.

"*Hijo!*"

"And there she is," Jack said, smiling as he turned to face a robust woman charging toward their booth. Her frizzy black hair bounced vigorously and her apron looked as though she had slaughtered many a pig out back. Jamie tried her best to hide the revulsion on her face as Jack stood, opened his arms, and accepted the woman's embrace. Apparently the apron of death didn't bother him at all.

"I hoped to see you again." She turned and shouted, "Luis, *mira!*"

The husband in question swiveled around and nearly fell from his stool. Jamie chuckled under her breath as the woman's hammered husband stumbled over and shook Jack's hand, then wrapped him in a sudden bear hug. Zamira rubbed Jack's shoulder, eager to fuss and fret over him. "Sam—" she began to say but trailed off when Jack gave her a sharp look.

Jamie looked away, uncomfortable and feeling as if she was intruding on their conversation.

The mention of Sam seemed to bother Jack. While the trio exchanged a few words, Jamie continued watching them, feeling awkward and more out of place in this homely bar. Jack hadn't tried to introduce her to these people he seemed to know well. She was a stranger in this place, as he was a stranger to her. She'd met him at a fishing lodge just over a week ago, and had sex with him last night. What the hell was she doing?

He admitted to not being in retail but didn't offer much of an explanation either. She stared at his broad back, overwhelmed with questions. It seemed odd that he would be here, right now, at the exact same time as she. Could he have something to do with why she was here? Suddenly, she felt sick to her stomach. What if Jack wasn't what she thought him to be? Maybe she had sex with someone who might hurt her when everything was all said and done. Her thoughts were so conflicting she didn't know which side to lean on. On one hand, he treated her with gentleness, opened doors for her, and complimented her. On the other hand, she knew nothing personal about him except in a physical sense.

"Sorry about that." Jack took his seat again, appearing the opposite of his usual cool and confident self. His smile seemed forced and he looked about the room as if distracted by something. Jamie detected a slight aloofness with his stiff body language as well, and it made her uncomfortable. "Zamira will bring our drinks shortly," he added, almost as an afterthought.

Jamie wondered if she should ask him some questions, try to get to know him a little better, maybe learn what his job was all about for real, where he lived, and who this Sam character was that made him react so strongly. But Jack didn't owe her anything. He certainly didn't owe her any explanations about his life. He'd saved her the trouble of getting ripped off by a young girl, and then asked her to join him for a drink. That seemed harmless enough, even though now she felt paranoid.

"I guess this is your go-to spot when you're in the city?"

Jack nodded and glanced around the room. "Zamira and I go way back. She's a tough old broad. One of the few I actually trust."

The woman in question stood behind the bar fixing their drinks. When her husband made a comment she didn't like, Zamira reached over and gave him a good smack across the face. Jamie's eyes widened and her jaw almost hit the table before she quickly turned her attention back to Jack. "I wouldn't want to be on the other end of that woman's temper."

He chuckled softly. "Neither would I. Poor Luis is half her size but he loves her. And mark my words, if anyone else treated him unfairly—well then there'd be hell to pay."

"But it's okay for her to just hit him like that?"

Jack's mouth tipped up at the corner. "It may seem like a cruel punishment, but I promise that he deserved it. He can be pretty vulgar when he's loaded."

Zamira finished up and wandered over with their drinks. "Here you go, lovies."

Jamie almost moaned aloud as she took the first tantalizing sip. "Oh my God, that's good. I've never tasted such a perfect cocktail."

Zamira's smile could shame the sun. "Only the best for my boy and his lady love."

Jamie blinked hard and darted a sharp glance at Jack, who simply shrugged. "I'm not his lady love." Her entire face heated as she tripped over the words, "Just a…an acquaintance."

"Pfft." Zamira clucked her tongue and shook her finger. "I know what I see, and my boy don't mess with no *puta*." As the old woman sauntered away, Jamie didn't know what to make of that. She hardly knew Jack, and even though she could kill to learn the woman's recipe for that mojito, now she felt put on the spot by being here with him.

Jack looked at her seriously. "So tell me how you managed to get a free vacation. A week in Havana isn't cheap, even at this time of year."

"What do you mean?"

"We're in the middle of hurricane season as you discovered yesterday. Not as many tourists around this time of year especially in the old town. Seems strange your friend would book a trip right now."

Right to the matter at hand. Jamie did her best to appear casual as she thought of what to say. They were just a couple of strangers having a drink, having met once before, who happened to have sex last night. And, there was a little matter of why she was here. "Well, my friend owed me some money and she thought giving me her vacation might lighten my mood. I have no idea why she booked the trip now, but it's gorgeous here. I've never been anywhere tropical. Hell, I've never left Canada before."

He chuckled, apparently content with her answer. "So what are your plans for tonight?"

Jamie shrugged, but the loaded question made her nervous. "I don't have any solid plans for tonight. Maybe find a nice place to eat."

"I know a few good places. I could make a few phone calls and get that set up. How about we have dinner together?"

Thankfully she managed to hide her immediate reaction to his question. She couldn't go out for dinner with him when she had a meeting at 5 p.m. "Uh…maybe that's a little too soon—"

He chuckled. "Too soon for what? Considering what happened last night, wouldn't dinner be expected, or was I just entertainment for you last night?"

Jamie's eyes widened and she almost choked on her drink. "Of course not. Is that what you really think?"

He shrugged and leaned back in his seat, hooked his arm over the backrest. The wolf expression on his face wasn't mistaken. "What would you like me to think?"

Jamie's heart hammered. She turned her attention to the view outside the dirty window, suddenly wishing she was somewhere else—like safely locked up in her room, alone, with her rubber dick. At least dildos didn't corner women and make them feel as if they'd taken a wrong turn somewhere, or overstepped their boundaries. *Why am I acting so strange?* "I'm sorry. Maybe I should leave—" Jamie cleared her throat and started to slide out from the booth, feeling more confused than ever, when Jack caught her forearm, halting her.

"I'm sorry. I didn't mean to upset you. Please…stay."

She released a frustrated breath and remained in her seat. "Okay. Just be aware that I came here for a vacation—not an interrogation."

There was something strange about the way he was looking at her, as if he couldn't figure her out, or maybe he wanted to ask something he shouldn't. "You're right." He smiled and it made her nervousness over his behavior settle down a minor degree. "If all goes as planned, I'll be retired after my meeting tonight."

"Retired already, and you're not even forty yet?" She blinked hard. Hearing those words from his mouth, when she'd busted her ass all of her life for a measly income, sounded wrong. How could someone retire at a young age without having to do some shady things? But then again, maybe she shouldn't believe him anyway. Her back stiffened and she itched to push her hair over her ear even though it wasn't in her face. She wasn't that much of an idiot not to suspect that his job had a lot more to do than retail, and that a name like Jack Daniels didn't seem right. "I guess congrats are in order." She lifted her glass and they clinked them together.

"Care to celebrate with me tonight?"

Perhaps it was time they part ways, for her peace of mind at least. She needed to be on her game this evening so the exchange happened without any hiccups. Besides, she couldn't let anything, or anyone, prevent her from seeing this mission to the end.

She sipped the last of her drink and smiled at him. "Thank you for the help today, and for the drink, *Jack*, but I should get going. Maybe tomorrow we'll have that retirement drink."

The challenging gleam in his eyes and curve of his sinful lips could've belonged to a snake. "Sure. Why not?"

Jamie smoothed the back of her dress and pushed out of the booth. Her hands shook and her throat felt tight as she walked toward the door. Before she touched the handle, she glanced over her shoulder. "Take care, Jack."

She couldn't help thinking that a man like him could probably charm a bull moose to shed its antlers. He might do more harm than good to a simple woman such as herself. As much as she felt an exhilarating attraction to him, she was afraid what consequences would come if she slept with him again. Could she handle a fly-by-night affair while on vacation and walk away unharmed?

"Jamie, wait."

She waited at the door with bated breath. Every hair on her body tingled as Jack slid out of the booth and strolled up to her like a man who owned the world. For the life of her she couldn't walk out the door. He may as well have thrown a line and hooked her damned soul. He was less than a foot away now, just like that night on the dock when he leaned in to kiss her. In the distance, standing behind the bar counter, she saw Zamira watching them intently, as if she knew something that they didn't. The lone man was also watching them. This made Jamie even more leery of being here.

"I have to admit, I'm having a hard time letting you walk away."

The look in his eyes almost made her cave. Maybe he was just a man who lived a solitary life, just like she was a lone woman who was almost virginal before he took her last night. He'd thoroughly cleared away the cobwebs in her panties.

That still didn't make her any less nervous.

"I'm not going home yet, Jack."

"I know. But something tells me this might be it…for us." He seemed nervous all of a sudden. "Last night was…."

"Last night was incredible." *There*. She said it, and she didn't blush.

His sudden smile made her feel all giddy inside. "Spend the night with me. You know you want to."

Something hot and funny flipped inside her stomach. She released a deep breath. "I'll think about it." And she left the bar before she changed her mind, realizing without a doubt that Jack Daniels wasn't who he seemed to be.

* * * *

At precisely 4:50 that afternoon, Jamie exited the hotel, wearing a bright red dress and red sandals. In her right hand she carried the briefcase. She had no idea what documents were locked inside, but she knew they were important. Her body trembled as she headed down the street toward the outdoor café. Every breath she took seemed to take effort. Monty had said the woman running the show wanted to remain anonymous, and this knowledge made Jamie so nervous she felt sick to her stomach. Why go to all this trouble over some documents, unless they were highly classified?

Wrapped around her left shoulder was her purse, and tucked under her arm was a particular book which was the key to the exchange.

It didn't matter that she wore the red dress or the red sandals, or even that she carried a briefcase. Any woman could show up wearing red, but who else would carry around a book about crocheting? At first she thought the idea to be completely ridiculous, but then again, this whole situation was insane.

The man would be watching her from one of the shops along the street, making sure she didn't try to pull any tricks. At exactly 5 p.m. if he didn't see a woman wearing red, and with that book on the table, there was no deal. If all went smoothly, he would simply walk up to her table, say hello, and ask if she had learned a new pattern. They would exchange one briefcase for another then go their separate ways. Once that was complete, then Jamie would wait for instructions to deliver the second briefcase before her departure in two days.

Jamie was determined not to screw this up. Then maybe, if Jack didn't get all weird on her, then she'd go for that celebratory drink.

It took her less than five minutes to walk to the café. She was already there waiting four minutes early. So far the mission had gone smoothly, thanks to her punctuality. Not once had she ever been late for work, she certainly wasn't going to be late for her final payment.

She found a table away from a populated section and discretely scanned the crowd. A few tables over she smiled at an elderly lady clad in a bright purple and red dress with matching sun hat. A moment later a few other brightly dressed women joined her for tea. As they mingled and laughed, Jamie focused on the other people at various tables. A man who looked close to her age sat alone, puffing on a fat cigar. Everywhere she looked, people mingled and smiled and enjoyed the beautiful day. Old cars whizzed by. Bicycles and horse-drawn carriages veered around pedestrians while stray dogs darted back and forth searching for scraps.

As five o'clock passed with no visit from her contact, she began to worry. As the seconds and then minutes ticked by, she constantly checked her watch.

When a waiter came to the table, she quickly shooed him away to make sure the contact hadn't noticed and changed his mind. As patrons left their tables and new arrivals took their seat, panic set in. Her heart hammered and her active imagination envisioned all the scenarios of what could go wrong. She scanned the vicinity for any man who carried a briefcase.

After an hour passed, Jamie became suspicious that maybe this was some kind of setup. People were looking at her now, maybe wondering why she was alone, without a drink or a meal in front of her. She called the waiter over and ordered a double margarita and pounded it back. The minutes ticked by, and then two hours passed. No man with a briefcase showed up.

By 7 p.m. and three double margaritas later, her vision began to blur. She no longer cared if the man showed up because she was probably screwed anyway. She was completely on her own in a foreign country with a briefcase containing documents she knew nothing about. There could be a million bucks in the briefcase, or a stash of heroin for all she knew. Terrified was an understatement. Yes, she had been desperate for money. Yes, she was willing to take on this crazy mission. But she did not agree to be somebody's lapdog. Anger, resentment, and fear set in as the sun made its slow descent over the rooftops.

It was at that moment that a shadow blocked the fading sunlight over her table. She glanced up and found a handsome, clean-cut man looking down at the book, with an odd expression on his face. His dark hair was pulled back into a ponytail, and he was dressed well in a button-down shirt and crisp slacks. His powerful cologne wafted over her as if he'd just doused himself only a moment before. Jamie immediately sat straighter and composed herself. She noted he wore some type of man purse on his shoulder. Perhaps this was the fashion for men in Cuba. Maybe that was his version of a briefcase—she couldn't be certain. Either way, he was looking at the crochet book.

"Can I help you?" She watched his face carefully. This must be him.

His dark eyes shifted from the book to her, and he smiled. "What is croch-e-ting?"

She almost laughed out loud by how he pronounced the word in his thick Spanish accent, but there was a problem. He was supposed to ask if she had learned a new pattern—not what the book was about.

"Um…it's basically knitting." She moved her hands in a motion that she hoped answered his question.

"Ah. Yes." He smiled and indicated the empty seat at her table. "May I?"

Jamie looked around as her heart leapt into her throat. *Breathe*. This wasn't the deal. "Perhaps you'd like to go somewhere else?" Somehow she managed to sound breathless as she said the words, although she was only terrified of screwing up the mission. It could very well be him and he was just making sure she played her part.

His gaze widened as well as his smile. "It would be my pleasure. Please...." He offered his hand and Jamie reluctantly accepted. Something told her to wait, to make the deal right here, but she couldn't fail. She *had* to go through with it. *Stay strong. You can do this. You're not a girl fresh out of high school.*

"Do you have it?" she pressed on, darting a glance behind her to make sure nobody followed.

His dark brows furrowed before he smiled and nodded. "I have *everything* you want, *Bella*."

Jamie allowed him to lead her to the next street where she guessed they would make the exchange around the corner. Perhaps it was best to be away from prying eyes, as well as the authorities, just in case the contents of the briefcase could get her arrested. From what she'd heard, Cuban prisons were far from accommodating.

They walked down two streets and finally entered a narrow alley with buildings that had yet to be renovated. It looked like a shady place to be conducting business, and when they rounded a corner and ended up in what looked like somebody's hideout, Jamie realized her mistake. She halted and took a step back. A cold dread gripped her.

"I think there's been a mistake."

"No. No, *Bella*," he urged and tried to grab her arm.

Jamie yanked her arm back, held the briefcase tight to her chest, and quickly turned around to head to a safe place. Perhaps a bar with people. Anywhere but here, and definitely not back to her table in case the real contact was waiting, and pissed that she'd screwed-up.

The man grabbed her arm, gripping hard, and spun her around. Before she could correct her footing, he grabbed her shoulders and shoved her against the wall.

Jamie dropped the briefcase and shoved against his chest. "Don't touch me!"

He pushed her back again and curled his fingers around the strap of her dress. The stifling scent of his strong cologne and the sickening odor of his putrid breath made her want to puke.

"How much, *Bella*?"

Disgusted, she shoved him hard and tried to break away, but he grabbed her by the neck. Stunned, Jamie's eyes widened. All the breath departed her lungs as she collided against the stone wall. She cried out in shock and terror as he pinned her against the wall with his forearm and roughly palmed her breast with his free hand. Jamie felt degraded, sick to her stomach, and helpless as he tried to break her willpower. She struggled as hard as she could, refusing to be a victim, but the weight against her neck held her to the spot. She choked on every sharp breath. Then he reached down, grabbing the hem of her skirt, and when his fingernails scraped along her thigh, survival mode kicked in.

She stamped her heel down onto his foot. He stumbled back with a loud grunt of pain, shifting his weight to the other leg. With all her might, she balled her fist and punched him right in the eye. While he was disoriented, Jamie grabbed the briefcase and made a mad dash farther into the alley.

"*Puta!*" he shouted behind her, then released a sharp whistle.

Running as fast as she could in heels, she glanced over her shoulder to find him and another guy giving chase. Not only did she make the mistake of walking off with this obvious hustler, now he had a partner, and she was heading further into the unknown.

She barreled around a corner and quickly took another turn into an alley barely wide enough for a person to walk through. Jamie pressed her back against the wall, hidden within the shadows and waited for them to pass. Once she knew they were gone then she could retreat back to the populated streets where she would be safer.

But as luck never worked in her favor, the first man moved into the opening at the beginning of the alley. He stood there panting, staring at her with savage victory in his eyes. Jamie suddenly knew that it didn't matter where she ran. She was in their domain. At their mercy. Tears filled her eyes when she realized, without a doubt, that she was hopeless. They would rape her, maybe even kill her. The deadly look in his dark eyes made her think it could be both. But she wouldn't just stand there like a helpless woman and let them force her body against her will. Not while she had breath left in her lungs and enough gall to kick them where it hurts.

While he still stood a safe distance away, her first instinct was to reason with him. "Please," she said, trying to maintain a steady, calm voice. "Just let me go. I won't say anything."

He tipped his head back and let out a throaty laugh. Her breath hitched and her stomach lurched with a sickening dread. The handsome man who'd approached her table only a moment before had turned into an ugly beast. He knew he had the upper hand. Despite her fear, she set the briefcase down beside her, balled her fists and took a protective stance. She wasn't going down without a hard fight.

At that moment a shot cracked behind him.

Jamie gasped as her attacker spun around and shouted at somebody in Spanish, although she didn't understand any of it. While his attention was averted, Jamie backed up farther into the alley, terrified that whoever was pulling the trigger out there would come for her next. Maybe an entire gang was after her. Why did she let Monty convince her to do this? He was the only one who would miss her if she was killed. She was completely alone now, and she had no way of reaching out to Jack for help.

No amount of money was worth losing her life over.

She heard a scuffle and another shot. Her attacker jumped back with fear in his eyes. He lifted his hands in defeat, begging for his life. Jamie stood there, frozen to the spot, as another man stepped out into the light, walked right up to her attacker and shot him in the face at point-blank range.

Jamie's breath hitched in her throat. Her ears rung hard as heat crept up her neck. She faltered on her heels and pressed her hand against the wall for balance, but it was too late. Her knees buckled and she slunk to the ground. The last thing she saw was the gunman walking into the alley, shrouded in shadow.

He was coming straight for her.

Chapter 7

Sam hoped his eyes were deceiving him as he had waited inside the café to watch over the exchange. But he knew better. When he saw Jamie approach the table, wearing a red dress and red sandals as instructed, at first he wanted to give her the benefit of the doubt. Red was a common color. It looked fantastic on her. But when she removed the book that was tucked under her arm and set it on the table, anger and betrayal superseded his disappointment.

He didn't want her to be the one. He wanted the timing of her vacation to be a coincidence, even if she did happen to have a briefcase.

The innocent woman from up north who happened to accept a free vacation from a friend was the very woman that was blackmailing them. Sam watched her like a hawk stalking a mouse as she took her seat at that table. He watched her every move, every facial expression, every nervous flick of her hair.

She was the coldhearted snake threatening to take Terry away from his children and Gabe away from the only happiness he'd ever had in his life. She had threatened Sam as well. His jaw clenched so hard he thought he'd crack a tooth.

He could've walked right up to her, snapped her neck, took the briefcase and left. He could've shot her from the rooftop of the building across the street. He could have slipped poison into one of her drinks. But he didn't. He couldn't grasp the fact that it was her. Sweet Jamie, so cute and kind, was the bad guy.

Not Jamie. He didn't want it to be Jamie.

He sipped his coffee in silent resentment as he watched her lose her composure. He had purposely called Gabe and told him to hold off an hour or two, so he could determine if she was with anyone. He sat up straighter and stared hard when he saw her wipe the tears from her eyes. He almost broke his coffee cup when that man approached her and led her away.

A woman who knew what she was doing wouldn't walk off with just anybody, and the terrified look in her eyes was enough confirmation that something was wrong. Jamie's reaction was of a confused and desperate woman who was given orders. He knew it like he knew something bad was about to happen to her. *Why did she have to make this job so difficult for me? Damn woman.*

Sam left the café the moment she and the stranger disappeared into the alley. He quickened his pace when he noticed a second man follow shortly behind. Sam knew Jamie was about to be set up for a robbery, and possibly a rape. A cold sliver of rage and fear made his instincts burst beyond control. It suddenly didn't matter that she was a part of this blackmailing. He wouldn't let those men take advantage of her, even knowing that she was taking advantage of him. How could she be so naïve taking off with that man? She had been given explicit, easy instructions to follow for the exchange. He grit his teeth as his anger for her would have to be taken out on those men.

He could make it easy on himself if he just let the guys go after her while he grabbed the briefcase, but he couldn't. Not now. Not when she'd managed to get under his skin.

Sam took a defensive stance as the second man realized he was being followed, turned around and rushed him, spearing his shoulder and taking him down hard. To Sam's surprise the small guy was stronger than he thought. They tumbled onto the cobblestones, each one fighting for the upper hand. But a street thug had nothing on a man who lived defying death every day.

He took a punch to the jaw, but it did nothing to stop the rage flashing red in his eyes. Sam grabbed the man's arm, twisted it behind his back and flipped him beneath him. He straddled his waist, gripped his hair with one hand, and pounded his face five times with the other. When the man could no longer see for the blood pooling into his eyes, and his lips swelled and spurted blood, he released him and stood back up.

He should kill him. He should shoot him in the chest and drag his body into the niche a few feet away, let the rats finish him off. But he was tired. He just wanted this to be over so he could go home and maybe live a normal life. He was done chasing after people, barely sleeping at night, and not knowing who he could trust. In the end, he just kept getting fucked anyway.

"Get the fuck out of here," Sam growled. He wasn't getting paid to kill these men, and he didn't want to waste his time or his bullets any more.

The guy shoved off the ground, ran a few feet away then pulled a handgun from his pocket. Sam shook his head. *So much for being generous.* As always, he was prepared for the worst and withdrew his Sig Sauer. He didn't want to kill him, but as the idiot raised his weapon, Sam shot him in the stomach without as much as a blink. The guy dropped his gun and slunk to the ground. A slow death was what he deserved for trying to take advantage of a woman, and for being an idiot.

Sam stood there looking down at him and shook his head. He would've let him live. The guy could've ran off and did something good with his life. Yet Sam felt no remorse for the choice he had made because the other guy had made his.

The guy tried to say something, but as he opened his bloody mouth, all that came from it was a soft gurgle before his head rolled to the side. Sam had finished caring the moment the guy pulled his gun on him.

As Sam stepped over the man's body, the first guy who had tricked Jamie shouted something he didn't understand. His eyes bulged, his face paled, and he swung his arms out in the air, apparently begging for forgiveness. Sam didn't really care what he said. He wanted to see the fear in his eyes. Wanted to hear him beg. He lifted his hand again, walked right up to him as he pled again for his life, and shot him in the left eyeball. He should've shot him in both just for looking at Jamie.

What he hadn't planned was how he'd explain himself to Jamie once she saw him. But luckily for Sam, she fainted first, hitting her chin hard on the stones. He stood there for a moment, just breathing. In and out. In and out. Contemplating what he should do with her, and with that briefcase.

Sam walked up to her and knelt down, wishing she didn't have to see that horrible scene, but glad he was able to stop the situation from getting worse. He gently touched her forehead, rubbed the dirt from her beautiful face. She had perfect eyebrows a shade darker than her blond locks, and her skin was so soft with that lush, golden tan. That was his downfall, because he couldn't stop touching her.

Then his gaze darted to the briefcase. He should take it and run. Everything would be over and he could return home back to what it was, how it's always been. But he wouldn't. He couldn't leave her like this. She did something to his heart that felt like indigestion. Was that love? Did love make a man want to puke when he thought he might lose her? He'd touched her, kissed her, made love to her. For that one amazing moment that took him away from everything he was used to, he couldn't let anyone hurt her, and he couldn't abandon her.

With his adrenaline still pumping hot, he retrieved the briefcase then bent down to gather Jamie's unconscious body in his arms. He held her close, breathed in the sweet floral scent of her hair, wishing he could be stronger than this. Why did she have to be so alluring?

As he rushed through the streets, she groaned and turned her face into his shirt. Her fingers gripped his arms. Relief flooded through him knowing her injuries didn't go beyond knocking herself out.

When he returned to the hotel, Sam brought Jamie straight up to his room and set her gently down on his bed. He was careful not to disturb her and slid the coverlet up to her chin. He immediately wetted a cloth in the sink and washed her face with cool water. Despite having a key to her room, he wanted her here, where he knew she was safe from anyone else. She may not be safe from him, but at least nobody else would touch her. That was a small relief at least.

She had a slight scrape on her chin where she'd hit the curb. A bruise had already begun to form on her delicate skin. He pulled out a lounge chair and sat next to the bed and watched her while she slept, at war with what he should do. He wanted to believe that she was innocent in all of this, but he was smart enough to know that women could be fickle creatures that lured men to their demise, all while smiling and laughing and acting like sweet little angels that tasted too good. He groaned aloud and leaned on his elbows, cradling his head in his hands. For the first time on a job, he felt like he had no control. He felt useless.

He contemplated calling Gabe and Terry and explaining the situation. Instinct told him that she may be in trouble. She may not be the woman behind the deal—not after being led into an alley by a street hustler. That whole situation didn't feel right. Either she was a pawn, or a victim, or she was the deadliest woman he'd ever put his hands on.

Something wasn't right, and it had nothing to do with his part of the mission. Perhaps she was desperate. He knew how hard it was to cope when you had very little money. Still, he couldn't assume anything at this point. He couldn't take any chances as he'd done before in the past. He almost fell in love with Wanda, even though it was his job to play the role of her lover. He had wanted to walk away from it all, but in the end, the lives of his brothers were more important than his needs. And after everything, she had her men drag him to the pigpen. Not a very loving woman. Wanda McCoy, the boss's second wife, had turned out to be the striking cobra that nearly killed him with her venom. Back then he thought he knew what love was, but now that Jamie blew into his life with a briefcase, he knew he was wrong.

Jamie was different by a long shot. He didn't think she was trying to trick him. He truly believed she was the one being used, but he couldn't trust himself to make the right choice either. It wouldn't be the first time the opposite sex duped him. Perhaps women were designed to hold a choke collar over his kind.

At Sharp Ridge Lodge she'd made him feel like his life could be different. That two people staring out over a moonlit lake had nothing to lose and everything to live for. Everything to hope for. So much to fight for. Maybe he was wrong. Maybe he knew nothing at all about women. But she looked stunning in that red dress.

He lifted his head and stared at her again, how her thick lashes fluttered from dreams. She seemed at peace, lying there, as if she was dead. Again, he imagined he could smother her with a pillow right now. He could put his hands on her throat and choke the life from her. It could be that easy.

But it isn't.

Sam wanted her very much alive, and naked, writhing on the bed beneath him. He wanted to skim his hands down her soft curves and pull her against him. He wanted to run his fingers through her soft golden hair as he did the night before. The wavy tresses felt like silk to his touch. And those eyes. Such a captivating mossy green, they seemed to look right through him. See him. As if she knew the real man within.

She could also be the most sly woman he'd ever met, and that was what prompted his decision. He would coax her, probe her, and do anything necessary to dig up the truth. And he would enjoy every second of it, even if it killed him in the end.

Police sirens shrieked in the distance. While she lay there in the grey void of consciousness, he stepped out onto his balcony and made a few phone calls. He needed to know who she really was, and his contacts would find out every sordid detail about her life within a few hours. Until then, he'd watch her and make damn sure that neither she nor the briefcase left his sight.

Once his calls were complete, he stepped back into the room and paused. His breath hitched, his brow arched, and a slight smile touched his lips as he watched Jamie, so beautiful in that red dress and heels, making his bed. He shook his head. The woman just witnessed a man shot at point-blank range in the face. She fainted from the gruesome sight and now she was concerned about his bedding.

He stared at her curvy ass as she bent over to tuck the top sheet under the corner of the mattress and flip the coverlet back over. It would take a while until her background was called in to him. What would he do with her in the mean time? A spike of arousal made his nostrils flare. His nuts ached for relief and his cock twitched with primal recognition. He could take her just like that, bent over his bed. Skim his hands over those beautiful ass cheeks and glide his cock into that hot, wet heaven.

Against his raging physical needs, he decided to talk to her. "You're awake."

Jamie spun around as if somebody had grabbed her shoulders and forced her around. Her eyes were as wide as marbles, her beautiful lips parted in a silent scream. "Shit, you scared m-me." She stared hard at him, perhaps trying to figure out how she got to his room. "How did...Where—?"

So she didn't know he killed those men. He breathed a little easier. "I saw you walk into that alley, then I heard the gunshots. I don't think those men will be bothering you again." He left it at that.

She nodded, visibly shaking from head to toes. Her face looked so pale it matched the paint on the walls. Her red-rimmed eyes were full of terror. As much as he wanted to tell her that she was safe now, he couldn't. He still had a job to do, whether he wanted to go through with it or not. *Damn this job. Damn this weakness for her!*

"Is that what you do when you're scared—make beds?" He couldn't help the humor in his tone. Sometimes it amused him to watch the emotional reaction when normal people witnessed death, when it was just another Tuesday for him. Still, he thought he should at least try to lighten the mood and maybe get some answers from her.

"I don't know what to do with myself." She plopped down on the edge of the bed and burst into tears.

That part he didn't know how to deal with. On one hand, he wanted to hold her and comfort her and ease her pain, yet he stood there like a rigid pole not knowing how to stop her crying. Every gut-wrenching sob made his stomach cinch and his knuckles tighten. That hair-raising sound made him feel sad, and useless. He cleared his throat, feeling more than a little awkward. Should he console her? Should he make her feel at ease before he had to kill her?

She held her head in her hands. Her golden hair spilled over her shoulders. "Oh, Jack, I don't know what I should do. What did I get myself into? This isn't what I...."

And she didn't even know his real name. For that he felt like an asshole. He deserved a full bore backhand across the eyeballs for that. Perhaps this insane situation was what they both deserved. Lies. Betrayal. But when they were together in that bed, everything was real.

He eyeballed her, his curiosity piqued by what she didn't finish saying. Maybe she was about to reveal the truth to why she was here, and who sent her. "I'm not sure what you mean…"

She lifted her face, eyes red and swollen, and for a moment his breath caught because she looked lovely. Sad, scared, and delicate. He swallowed. He wanted to kiss her eyes and make them wet with passion—not sadness.

Something happened in his chest that he didn't like. Like that time he was waterboarded by a rival hitman in Egypt. He couldn't breathe now as he couldn't breathe that day, so long ago. Sam had walked into the apartment to find his target was already dead. Before he realized his mistake, a sack was thrown over his head from behind, and he was dragged into the room. That was the first and only time he'd been careless. Death was within reach as his lungs fought to control his breath while the water was forced into his mouth. Just when he thought it was over, as his body started to sag in defeat, the door burst open and he heard shouting through the sac over his face.

It was Norman the Norwegian who'd gotten him out of that mess. Apparently three rival hitmen had taken the job, and when the first shooter got the target, he decided to take Sam out at the same time. While Sam and Norman were not exactly friends, they had a mutual understanding and respect for each other. He regretted having to kill Norman in that bathroom like some cheap drug deal gone wrong, but the big Norwegian left him no choice.

Sam had a choice with Jamie. He could kill her and take the briefcase, or he could keep an eye on her and see where this ended. If she wasn't alone in this, which he suspected, then he needed to get the real villain. Maybe he could help Jamie get through this without getting hurt. But he needed answers.

"You can tell me anything," he pressed on, his thoughts back to the situation at hand. "You're safe with me." *Quit lying to her.* He grit his teeth. *You know what you have to do.* He had to force himself to breathe evenly, when all he wanted was to explode and either punch the wall or push himself inside her.

Jamie shook her head, a defeated expression on her face. She shoved up and off the bed. "I can't do this. This is fucking crazy." She seemed to be fighting with some inner demon as she bent to grab the briefcase, and Sam realized that if she left his room right now, that would be it. Whatever her role was in this fucked-up situation, if he let her leave and go through with the exchange, then he'd have to kill her. He'd *have* to kill her.

He couldn't let her go, not when all their lives and their freedom were at stake. Now he suddenly wished he'd never met her at that lodge. Jamie

Fields had become an itch that he couldn't scratch, a thorn in his ass, a drink for his thirst.

Fuck!

"Wait." He walked up to her, feathered his fingers through her hair and tilted her head back. As she gasped in surprise, Sam brought his lips to hers and kissed her. He wanted to keep her here and shut her up at the same time. He couldn't be sure if it was his frustration with the situation, or his feral attraction to her, or both, that made him ravage her, but he couldn't help himself.

He had to have her. Right now. Fuck the consequences.

* * * *

Jamie's head spun.

She had just witnessed a murder, and had nearly been killed herself, and yet, being in Jack's arms, having him kiss her with abandon, and hold her with such raw need shoved reality right out the door. All her fear and frustration and desperation vanished while he touched her as if he owned her.

The briefcase dropped to the floor beside them as she lifted her arms and wrapped them around his neck, holding him tighter. *God forgive me, but I want him inside me. I need him inside me. Now.*

Driven by lust, and maybe even fear, she dug her nails into his back, scraped all the way down and around his lean hips, then violently tore his zipper down. In seconds she had his pants around his ankles and her hands on his dick.

They both panted and moaned. Jack looped the straps of her dress around his fingers and peeled the garment down her body, taking her panties with it in one smooth sweep. Jamie whimpered, her body aflame as his fingers slipped between her wet pussy lips to tease her sensitive clit. She ground her hips against his finger, pushing harder while he kissed her, already on the edge of a wild climax.

"This is how you should be treated by a man—ruining your lipstick, not your mascara." He slid his fingertip farther down and teased that dark place nobody else ever had the nerve to touch. Jamie's high-pitched cry shrieked through the room as she shuddered and quaked with every torrid touch.

"Why do I want you so much?" she moaned, as he trailed kisses over her chin and down to her breasts. The tears she had tried so hard not to cry, slipped down her cheeks. *Just breathe. Forget about everything else. This is what you need.*

"Tell me to stop," he murmured between kisses.

"*No. Please.* Don't stop."

Their lips met again and all thought of the previous hour vanished, replaced with a need for nothing but pleasure. She needed this. Needed to feel loved and safe and forget what tomorrow would bring.

He kissed her as though his sole purpose was to satisfy her every whim. Her entire body tingled, nipples tight, the apex of her thighs wet and aching for more. His luscious lips, so soft and delicious, set her aflame as he kissed her mind blank. She succumbed, weightless in his arms and let the mating call take its course.

With one hand on her hip, Jack moved the other up along her ribcage to circle each aroused nipple through her bra. She shuddered, grinding against him. Empowered by his arousal, Jamie stroked his cock with desperate abandon.

With a rough moan, he reached behind and unhooked her bra, nearly ripping it off her, then he swung her up in his arms to place her gently onto the bed. "If you keep touching me like that, your vacation will never end," he growled, and buried his face between her tits.

Jamie moaned and feathered her fingers through his curly hair, holding him there as he bit her nipples. She wanted the exchange to end, but not her time with Jack. She didn't want to think about never seeing him again. Couldn't bear to imagine not feeling his body taking hers, gentle and slow and fast and deep. She feared her attraction to him, her need to have him again and again, as if her body had been created for his touch.

She gripped his shoulders, turned on by the play of muscle she felt there, bunching and flexing as he set to work making her numb with lust. His deep, guttural growl made her pulse race as he skimmed his hand up her torso, the heat of his palm soft and erotic on her excited flesh.

As Jack slid off the bed and stood at the foot, staring down at her with a smirk on his luscious lips, Jamie suddenly felt mortified by her nakedness. A blush pinched her cheeks. He'd seen her naked before, but the bright chandelier hanging over his bed made everything more visible. Every flaw more enhanced.

"Don't be shy. You're beautiful," he murmured. His words soothed her nerves, but his slow, almost evil smile disturbed her. *Why is he looking at me like that?* And before she could question what he was about, Jack squatted down at the foot of the bed and removed her heels. His devilish expression made her push up on her elbows and watch, mortified yet curious as he traced his fingertip along the curve of her foot.

She sucked in a sharp breath. "*Oh...wow.*" How could a foot elicit that much erotic pleasure? She quivered and whimpered as he gently kissed the sensitive area at the arch of her foot—only there, where the sensitivity was too acute for words.

"Did you know your feet were that sensitive?"

"God no. Not like that," she purred.

"Nerve endings should not be ignored."

Jamie giggled and shuddered again as he kissed and tickled another scintillating path. "If I would've known this, I would've had you on the dock, and every day after *that*," she cried out. Good thing her feet weren't too ticklish or she might've kicked him in the face. *No, nerve endings should never be ignored.*

He chuckled, and the vibration on her foot sent more convulsions right between her legs. She closed her eyes and reveled in this new and wicked attention. Slowly and provocatively, Jack kissed up her calves to the crook of her knees. Every inch of quivering flesh was definitely not ignored as he worked his way up her body. She thought she'd ruin the mattress she was so wet, or at least become a part of the bed itself, so heavy she felt—heavy yet weightless at the same time.

She feathered her fingers through his hair again as her hips gyrated beneath him. He took her nipple in his mouth and rolled the aching tip between his teeth and tongue. She cried out and raked his scalp with her nails.

"Dammit, Jack, I'm really beginning to like you."

He glanced up, his sexy eyes drowsy with lust, and Jamie knew then and there that she didn't want to let him go. Even if tonight was their last night together, she'd enjoy every breathless moment. It was in that moment of reflection when she realized that *like* wasn't a strong enough word. What she felt for Jack was much stronger than that, and it terrified her.

She wrapped her arms around his neck and ground her hips against his burgeoning erection. He pulled away with a dark smile and worked his way back down her body. Feverishly aroused, Jamie wished he'd be quicker and take her already. But he sat back at an angle, as if he had all the time in the world to please her. Propped on one elbow, he parted her legs with his free hand, his eyes feasting on her bared pussy. When his head dipped and his ravenous tongue delved around her clit and down her wet lips, Jamie thought she'd fly off the bed. She gripped the bedding and gasped as he ravaged her with his tongue, turning her body to liquid and her mind to mush.

He took his time, delving deeper, applying more pressure. Jamie didn't know how much more she could take.

"I need you inside me, please, Jack."

"Soon," he said. "You're almost there." He replaced his tongue with his finger and in a slow, agonizing rhythm he stroked her...around and around...each deft strike making her hips rise a little higher. He stared at her face, watching her expressions of joy and ecstasy as he continued strumming her without a lick of shame. Heat crept up her neck and face, a sure prelude to orgasm. She cried out and her hips arched, almost of their own will as the wave rocked her. With a deep moan, Jack slowed his pace but continued teasing her mercilessly.

Jamie panted, lying limp on the bed now, her entire body buzzed and numb. Amazed that he could control her so easily, she blushed and looked away from his bold gaze. She smiled shyly, aware of how she must have looked coming undone so easily. Jamie was a strong woman, but here was this stranger who boldly spread her thighs and tasted her as if he had every right.

The moment Jack reached up to undo the top button of his shirt, Jamie scooted onto her knees, ready to take over. She smiled when he chuckled and proceeded to undress him quickly. Her patience had worn thin long ago. The last button gave way and she reached up to peel the shirt over his shoulders, letting it pool at his feet beside his already discarded pants and boxers.

His brown skin, lightly dusted with dark hair, captivated her. She sucked on his nipples, teasing and nibbling, just as he had done to her. His rough moan excited her. While she toyed with him, Jack reached down and took the weight of her breasts in his hands, kneading and pinching her nipples.

She swirled her tongue around his nipple before she bit down with a measure of force. His sudden jerk and grunt of pain gave her instant pleasure.

The challenge she saw in his eyes excited her. She took him in hand and stroked his shaft more forcefully, convincing herself that even though he was bigger than a decent man should be, she'd use every inch of him, again. His cock was darker than the rest of his body, which was intriguing and appealing, especially when her fingers looked so white wrapped around him, a stark and beautiful contrast. She kissed and licked around his head, delighted as he groaned and pumped his hips forward. The ache between her legs deepened, pulsing in unison with each stroke of her hand and kiss from her lips.

Jack skimmed his hands up her arms and gathered her hair in one hand, holding it to the side for a better view. He growled when she gripped the base of his shaft and sucked his head into her mouth, taking him down as far as she could. Her throat tightened, triggering a heady pulse between her legs that she could no longer ignore.

As he reached for the condoms on the nightstand, Jamie shook her head. "No. I want to feel you."

Jack blinked, obviously taken back by her words. "Are you sure?"

"Yes." She'd never let a man come inside her before. Never trusted a man enough to take it that far. But she wanted Jack to have her completely. She wanted to feel everything.

Jack's eyes seemed to darken with lust and something else, as he gripped her hips and pulled her to him while he remained standing at the side of the bed. Her ass hung slightly over the edge of the mattress. She bit her lip and gasped in pleasure as he guided his naked length along her slick pussy lips, instigating a fevered need to feel him deep. To forget about what waited beyond the door and find ecstasy—raw, naked ecstasy.

Jamie released a startled breath and gripped the bed linen, that first slow thrust almost painful, as it had been the first time. Her eyes widened and he held still, allowing her body to succumb, and to eventually beg for more.

Then he fed her the rest.

They both moaned in unison.

Filled was an understatement, Jamie decided, as she moved in tune to him. She stared at his piercing eyes while he penetrated her slowly, madly, deeply. She raked her nails along his forearms and met his thrusts, already feeling the rush drawing near.

Gently, he stroked her inner thighs, applying pressure with the pads of his thumbs. The gesture made something unravel within and the flutter of heat in her belly deepened. His fingers surged higher, still circling, massaging, and driving her wild, until he pressed the pad of his thumb against her clit.

Jamie closed her eyes and rocked with him, her breath short and sharp, feeling as though she floated above the mattress in a fiery inferno.

The intensity heightened as Jack quickened his pace, filling her deeply, owning her body. The sound of their bodies smacking together resounded throughout the room.

He lifted her bottom, raising her higher, thrusting deeper, and it was Jamie's undoing. She arched and cried out. Jack lifted her higher in his arms and kissed her passionately, still thrusting hard. Sweat beaded off his brows. Three more deep pumps and his hips stilled, his breath quickened, and he found his own shuddering climax.

It was during the blissful aftermath, as they lay limbs entwined, nothing but the sound of heavy breathing in the room, that her cell phone rang. Jamie's lids fluttered lazily, not quite back to reality yet, but after the third ring, she jerked up in bed.

Only one person would be calling, and she didn't want to answer. How could she explain what happened today while Jack was right next to her? She dared a glance over her shoulder. His eyes were closed, chest moving evenly with each breath.

Jamie picked up the cell, her eyes still trained on Jack, and lowered her voice. "Yes?" His lids didn't flicker at all.

"How did it go today?" Monty asked, his voice high with expectation.

Jamie's stomach swirled as the vision of those two men came to mind. She turned away from Jack and whispered, "It didn't."

"What? What the fuck happened?" Monty's suddenly shrill voice echoed loud through the receiver.

Her chin quivered and her hand holding the receiver trembled. She cleared her throat, nervous that Jack might hear their conversation. "Uh, now really isn't a good time, Mom. I'll call you later." That man would've raped her, but somebody killed him. Somebody came toward her after killing that man, but thank God Jack had heard the commotion and came to her rescue.

But how did he get past the man with the gun?

"What the hell is going on?"

"Nothing," she said quickly. "I'll call you first thing in the morning. I promise. Love you," she added, tasting the bitter truth of that word toward a mother she'd never known.

Jamie hung up the phone as the weight of her responsibility pushed heavily on her shoulders. The anonymous woman probably didn't care that Jamie could've been killed today. All that mattered was the briefcase. She stared at it and wondered if what was inside would be her undoing. Even if she wanted to know what lay within, she had no code to open it. Maybe she was better off not knowing anyway.

She glanced at Jack again, only half relieved that his eyes were still closed and his soft snores filled the room. But it didn't settle her fear that her job still wasn't complete. There could be hell to pay, and she didn't know exactly what happened earlier. If Jack saw her come into the alley and heard the shots, how did he manage to get her back here without getting shot at?

She settled back under the covers and cuddled up to him, needing his warmth and his strength. Their bodies fit together as if by design. That thought scared her. How could she feel safe in his arms and in his bed when she still didn't really know him? How could she be falling in love with a stranger?

For a long while she lay there wide awake, wondering if she told Jack why she was here and what was happening, if he'd help her.

Chapter 8

As Jack showered early the following morning, Jamie decided she had better call Monty back before the boss lady began to worry.

A woman answered on the first ring. "Hello, Jamie. What happened with the meeting yesterday?"

Jamie swallowed hard, sensing something terrible on the immediate horizon. "Where's Monty?" The woman on the other end laughed, and Jamie realized with dread that this must be the woman who set up the mission, the same voice she'd spoken with when she first took on the job. "Why are you answering Monty's phone? What have you done with him?"

"Monty will be just fine as long as you do your part of the job. When I give instructions, I expect them to be followed implicitly."

Her hand holding the phone began to tremble as her heart skipped a jagged beat. What had she done? Monty could be in grave danger, and here she was, in Jack's room, after spending another wonderful night with him.

She wanted to scream at this woman who put her in this dangerous situation, but instead Jamie forced herself to breathe steady. Freaking out wouldn't do Monty any good. She'd never forgive herself if he got hurt because she failed to do her part of the mission, and as much as she didn't want to explain herself to this woman, she knew she had to. "The wrong man showed up yesterday. I swear it wasn't my fault. I went to the café at the exact time as I was supposed to and I followed your instructions to the T. A man showed up carrying a bag, we exchanged a few words, and he led me to believe that we had to make the exchange away from people. He and his buddy turned out to be hustlers and they would've robbed and possibly raped me—"

"The briefcase?" the woman snapped.

Jamie glared at the phone as tears welled in her eyes. *Don't cry now. Lift your chin and show this bitch that you can be tough.* "Don't worry, your precious briefcase is safe. What the hell is going on? Tell me that Monty is okay."

"Did you see who shot those men?"

"No." Her cheeks heated. "I've never witnessed a murder up close before. I fainted, right as the guy was walking toward me."

There was a long pause. "What happened when you woke up? The shooter was gone?"

She lifted her chin and squared her shoulders, although the woman on the other end couldn't see that Jamie had had enough of this. "I want to talk to Monty."

"I'm sorry but that's not possible."

The carefree, posh tone of the woman's voice made Jamie grit her teeth. "If you don't put Monty on the phone, then I won't go through with this!" She never should've accepted this mission, especially if it put her best and only friend in danger. If Monty got killed because of her, she'd never forgive herself.

"Oh, you will, if you want to see your friend alive again." The sharp tone ripped right through Jamie's heart. There was no getting away from this now, she was certain.

The tears she tried to force away slipped down her cheeks. This was getting worse by the minute. "A man rescued me. I'm here with him right now."

"Really?" The voice seethed through the receiver. "What do you know about this man?"

Jamie's eyes widened and her heart stilled. "What do you mean?"

The woman's voice took on a hard tone. "Very coincidental that this man, who you know nothing about, rescued you just as you were about to switch briefcases?"

"Oh my God," Jamie whispered out loud. She had wondered last night how Jack managed to rescue her without getting hurt, or at least, shot at. What if this woman was right and Jamie's earlier suspicion of him turned out to be true? How could she be so stupid? She should've put the pieces together when he said he was retiring on the same night as the first exchange was supposed to take place. He could be the one she was originally supposed to meet.

A cold clasp of terror gripped the back of her neck.

Jamie stepped closer to the curtains at the opening of the balcony and peeked into the room. The shower was still running. Steam billowed out from the bathroom into the bedroom. "Do you think it's him? I admit I was a little suspicious at first, but he doesn't seem like—"

"Seem and *is* are two very different things, Miss Fields. Believe me, I know what men are all about. They gain your trust so you give your body to them. That's all they want. Do you know anything else about him to make you think otherwise?"

No. She felt strangled by the words. Dissected like an animal. The woman was right. She didn't know him. She didn't know anything other than how his body felt against hers. How when he looked at her with those sexy eyes, she felt unraveled. She really thought he wanted her, that maybe, just maybe, they could have something. She closed her eyes and exhaled. *I'm such a fool.* All over again, the terror hit her, and she felt betrayed, by Jack and by herself, and also by this woman who had all the control. A woman she'd never even met.

Had Jack been using her all along? Her gaze darted to the briefcase. What was so important about the contents inside?

"What do you want me to do?" Even though she didn't trust this woman as far as she could spit, right now, Monty's safety meant more than anything.

"Get out of there, that's what I want you to do. Make the exchange and disappear. Wait for me to call you, and stay away from that man. Monty's life depends on you."

Jamie closed her eyes and fought the sting of tears as her entire body turned cold. She didn't even give the woman the pleasure of an answer. She hung up, cursing the bitch under her breath, and rushed for the briefcase. The shower was still running. The soft lilt of Jack singing in the shower should've been a happy sound, but it only made her wonder what kind of man she had fallen in love with.

What kind of people was she dealing with?

She was terrified that something bad would happen to Monty if she didn't complete her part of the mission, at the same time her heart ached knowing that her time with Jack last night would be her last.

Jamie paused as she gripped the doorknob. It felt wrong to leave him like this again, without saying something, but she had no choice. She didn't believe Jack was a man out to get her, but she couldn't take any chances. If Monty wasn't safe, and the woman wanted her to leave, then she would. She didn't give her any other choice.

With regret and her heart heavy with sadness, Jamie slipped out the door as silently as she could and ran for her room. In five minutes she had her suitcase packed, quickly changed from the red dress and high heels into a tank top, shorts, and comfortable sandals, and managed to exit the hotel without being seen.

She felt like a damsel in a Bond movie. Or maybe the villain's assistant. Nothing was what it seemed, and everything was slipping through her fingers like rain water through a cracked eave. Only the water was leaking through the outer walls and ruining the foundation of her life.

Her heart hammered as she flagged down the same young man on the bicycle taxi who had approached her before. Several blocks away, he brought her to a backpacker's hostel discreetly nestled between two huge stone buildings that suited her situation perfectly. The hostel was overcrowded and well hidden—as she needed to be. She paid cash for the room, used a fake name, and settled in to wait for the woman's call.

All she wanted was to get this over with and go home. She thought about what Monty must be going through. Visions filled her head of him tied up in a basement, or being held in the trunk of a car. She didn't even want to think about Monty already being dead. He couldn't be. And as much as she wanted to leave that briefcase in this room and leave it all behind, she knew she couldn't.

Just when she was beginning to have feelings for a stranger, a man who broke his way into her heart, this shit had to happen.

The phone rang twenty minutes later just as she was starting to nod off, exhausted from the nonstop excitement since she'd gotten here. The woman gave her new instructions on where to go and how to get there, and let her know what time she would be expected. As she wrote down the information, her mind wandered back to that hotel room and what her lover was doing. Did he try to look for her or was she just a passing excitement for him? So many questions chased each other in her mind that her head ached with resentment, fear, and anger. When she ended the call, she got up, grabbed the briefcase, and headed to the new destination. There was no time to gain her composure. This was it.

Plaza Vieja was packed at noon. Children played around the old fountain in the center of the square. A group of teenagers wearing backpacks stood admiring, or maybe questioning the meaning of the sculpture of a bald woman, holding a huge fork, sitting atop a rooster at one corner of the square. Every table at the outdoor restaurant was filled with happy, smiling people. Even a few cats and dogs wandered freely through the open space, hoping to catch a morsel of food.

Everybody was happy, except for Jamie. She was a frazzled mess, thrown into a dangerous world much different than anything she'd lived through before.

Potted palms and other shrubs dotted the cobblestones in the open square, as well as behind the columns of the open main floor of the buildings surrounding the plaza. Although all four sections of buildings were connected, every façade was painted a different color. Yellow. Peach. Blue and beige. Even orange.

So much beauty to look at and listen to. Too bad she couldn't enjoy it.

Jamie wandered around the plaza pretending to take in the beautiful views, all the while watching everyone around her.

She smiled as she passed a man leaning against one of the huge columns playing a saxophone. The sound was so heart wrenching, it made her think of Jack and all the mistakes she'd made since being here. She nearly cried right in front of the musician.

At 1 p.m. she entered the photo gallery as instructed. On a wrought iron bench in front of a huge panoramic view of the plaza, sat a man with his back to her, and a briefcase on the seat beside him.

This is it. Taking a deep breath, Jamie squared her shoulders, summed up her courage, and approached the bench. Her eyes widened, but she said nothing when she recognized the man from Zamira's bar. He had been watching her from his seat the day before, while she and Jack had a mojito. Maybe he had been following her right from the beginning. Yet another coincidence since coming to Havana. Jack had said he didn't know this man, but maybe he did. Maybe he'd been lying to her all along.

She couldn't screw this up. Monty's life was in her hands now.

"Beautiful picture, isn't it?" She set her briefcase beside his and took a seat.

The man nodded and stood. "It sure is." His deep voice slithered over her skin as if his words were a threat. He grabbed her briefcase and left without another word.

She lowered her head and had to catch her breath. Shaking, Jamie pulled the other briefcase close to her hip and stared at the photo for a long while. She felt lost and alone. She had a feeling this whole exchange wouldn't end as she thought it might. It felt as though she were about to drive off a cliff and there wouldn't be anyone around to save her.

* * * *

Sam stepped out of the shower and toweled himself dry, relaxed and content in the decision he had made. He wanted to help her. He didn't know how, but he knew that it was the right thing to do. He felt it in his bones. She wasn't the villain here, somebody else held the power over her. If he made arrangements to switch briefcases now and followed her once she had the money, then he'd get their true target.

He wondered if she even knew what was in the briefcases. Did she know she was about to trade proof of the McCoys dealings in exchange for ten million bucks? If she didn't, then she was being completely blindsided. He needed to coax the truth out of her before it was too late.

The moment he stepped out of the bathroom, the words he was about to say to her died in his throat when he noticed she was gone, and his room had been ransacked. He leaned heavily against the bathroom doorframe and stared at the upturned room.

His suitcase lay on the floor, its contents scattered everywhere. The mattress had been lifted from the bed and lay half on the box spring, half on the floor. The bedding he and Jamie had made love on lay in a heap at the foot of the bed. Every drawer in the dresser and doors of the small armoire were open. A couple of the drawers lay on the floor as well. How the hell didn't he hear all of that?

Good thing he kept the other briefcase at Zamira's.

He shook his head, ripped the towel off his waist, and whipped it at the wall. It slid down and landed on the bedside lamp, knocking it off balance. The lamp tumbled off the nightstand and bounced off the floor; the bulb smashed into pieces. Sam didn't care. The place could burn down with everyone in it. Having Jamie leave yet again and rip through his stuff like a common thief was probably the hardest gut-punch he'd ever had.

How could I be so stupid?

Fueled by anger, he called his contact, fully expecting the background on her to be substantial. But as he listened to the officer on the other end, he realized with dread that Jamie Fields was just a regular woman who really did work as a housekeeper. A few years ago the cops had her on their radar for suspicion of selling cocaine, but she was never caught or charged for anything. She didn't even have a speeding ticket. She had no known relatives and suffered a horrible past in the foster system. Sam understood, to a certain degree, how lonely she must feel. Even though he had his Auntie Rose, he still understood the loneliness of not really knowing his parents; of having a hard time trusting people because of feeling left behind by the ones you love the most.

Now he didn't know what the hell to do. If she wasn't a criminal, then why would she rip apart his room? Maybe whoever she was working for discovered that he was here and notified her of his identity. That wouldn't be good. If she learned his true identity, and what he was capable of, well then she'd probably feel betrayed and used and outraged. Maybe she was running into something that could get her killed before he could stop her.

He dressed quickly and retrieved his gun from the locked case, slipping it into the back of his pants. As he headed down the hallway toward her room, his cell phone rang—it was Gabe.

He didn't answer the call, and let it go to voicemail as he slipped the spare key card through the slit and entered Jamie's room. He scoured every inch of the place only to find she'd disappeared. Not a trace of her had been left behind except the flowery smell from her hair. He stood there like a fool, not sure if he missed her or if he hated her, as he checked the message Gabe left for him.

"One p.m. at Plaza Vieja, in the photo gallery. If you can't go through with it, then I will."

Then I will...

Every muscle in his body flared to life. He imagined Gabe standing behind his beautiful Jamie and raising his gun to the back of her golden hair. "Like hell you will," he growled.

Sam checked his watch. He had fifteen minutes to get there. "*Fuck.*" He ran from the room, took the stairs at a breakneck speed, swearing to God that if Gabe killed her, he'd break his face. Jamie was his responsibility, and his alone. He hoped it wasn't too late as he charged out of the hotel front door and ran down the street.

This was his mission—not Gabe's. Not once did any of the boys have to take over Sam's job. It pricked at him like a needle in his gums that Gabe doubted him. The fucker had no right to step on his toes like that. Sam knew what he was doing. Just because he happened to sleep with her, twice, didn't mean he couldn't still do his job...if he had to. But he didn't want to.

The plaza was busy as Sam slowed his steps, coughed hard, and surveyed the crowd. Considering his years of being a smoker, his chest was tight and he struggled to stay on foot. Perhaps it was time to give up that nasty habit and finally breathe steady.

Tourists and locals milled about. Kids used the square as their playground. A dog sniffed his knee and barked up at him. He rubbed the mutt's head and made his way toward the photo gallery.

As he walked up to one of the columns flanking the doorway, Gabe stepped through the opening carrying the other briefcase. He didn't notice Sam standing there by the column, and Sam didn't alert him to his presence. He watched as Gabe glanced over his shoulder, then quickly darted around the column. It was then that Jamie exited the same door carrying the briefcase with the money. She picked up her pace, darting around people, yet keeping close for safety, her frantic gaze watching everyone around her. But she didn't see either of them.

When Gabe followed her away from the crowd and toward an alley, Sam followed as well. He kept his distance as they ventured deeper into the heart of Old Havana. Children laughed and whizzed between the adults. A dog chased the children in a clumsy gallop as Sam chased after Gabe who chased after Jamie.

Yesterday Jamie had said that she still had a few days left of her vacation. But after the failed exchange between her and Sam, he wouldn't be surprised if she'd be gone after today. He couldn't let her out of his sight, and he couldn't let Gabe get his hands on her either.

Jamie waved down a taxi and opened the back passenger door. Sam sucked in a sharp breath, every muscle tense as Gabe reached into his pocket and withdrew his handgun. *No. Don't do it.* Sam ran to him, his exhausted lungs screaming in protest, and yanked his own piece from the back of his pants. He whacked the handle of his pistol against the back of Gabe's head just as he pulled the trigger.

The bullet smacked into the wall behind the taxi at the same moment as Jamie shut the passenger door. The old Studebaker sped off.

People screamed and scattered in the streets as Sam managed to grab Gabe from behind the moment his legs crumbled beneath him. As Gabe's heavy body slumped to the ground, Sam dragged him over the curb to lean his back against the wall. Sam stood back and tucked his gun into his pants. He bent down and murmured to an unconscious Gabe, "Sorry, bud, but you left me no choice."

He immediately called Zamira to send Luis to pick him up.

Sam grabbed the briefcase out of Gabe's limp hand and shot off down the road after the taxi. One block over, just as Jamie's taxi took a corner, Sam noticed a group of scooters sitting outside of a bar. He hopped onto the nearest one, ignoring the shout from somebody inside, and started the engine. Like a bullet firing from a chamber, Sam shot off after the woman, who may or may not be a criminal, who managed to make him fall in love with her.

Damn woman. How she managed to grip his heart and make it pound like a drum, just for her, should be a goddamned crime.

He veered through traffic but the taxi gained momentum. Determined to reach her before it was too late, Sam pushed the scooter to its max. The little engine screamed in protest as he jumped onto a sidewalk to barrel closer to the old Studebaker. A woman screamed, throwing her grocery bags in the air. A head of lettuce whipped against his face, but it did not deter him. Nothing would get in his way, until a woman and a stroller ventured out onto the sidewalk.

Sam's eyes bulged as he neared the stroller. The woman, talking to somebody beside her, had no idea what was about to happen. Sam veered to the side, just as the woman turned her head and realization struck home. She screamed and pulled the stroller back. But it was too late for Sam. As he'd turned back onto the street, to save the baby, a delivery truck pulled out in front of him. There was no time to stop.

He shifted to the side. The bike bounced off the pavement and skidded toward the truck. Still holding on and gritting his teeth as sparks flew up, Sam and the scooter slid to a heart-pounding stop underneath the truck.

Exhaust filled the air around him. He thought the fumes might also be making tears well up in his eyes as he watched Jamie's taxi take the corner and disappear. Lying there under the delivery truck like a fool with his legs still clinging to the scooter, Sam closed his eyes and shook his head. He failed to catch her. He hated failure.

She was gone. It could take days, weeks, or months to find her now, and by then the briefcase could be long gone. It might very well be in someone else's hands already. Nothing was certain. But Sam was beyond terrified that she could be in grave danger.

Ashamed and angry, he picked the scooter up and pulled it out from under the truck. The driver, hanging out of his window, shook his fist at Sam. "*Idiota!*"

Sam sighed. He certainly wasn't going to argue with the man. *Yeah, I know*. He headed back to where he'd left Gabe. The left side mirror hung by a couple of wires. Most of the paint had become part of the pavement now. The warped front wheel made the bike bounce as Sam drove the thing back in complete defeat. People stared at him as if he were some kind of lunatic, driving a barely operable, mashed-up scooter, with a briefcase in one hand. But he didn't care. He'd lost her. Jamie Fields was gone.

He pulled the scooter up a short walk away from the bar where he'd stolen the machine, and dropped the thing right onto its side. When he rounded the corner, he found Luis helping Gabe up from the street. As Gabe's eyes darted to Sam, he gave him a sheepish grin. The meaning behind Gabe's glare should've at least maimed him as Sam walked over holding the briefcase.

"I should've known you'd do that to me, thinking with your dick all the time. I'll get you back for that, mark my words." Gabe rubbed his head and winced.

"I deserve it. And now that she got away with the money, I accept whatever death you and Terry might have planned for me."

Luis stood to the side looking bored. Sam figured he was probably thirsty, then suddenly wondered how much he knew about Zamira's connection to them.

Gabe yanked the briefcase out of Sam's hand, jolting him back to the scene. "You'd think with all the years you've been in this business, you'd be smart enough to put a tracking device on that woman." Gabe started walking back in the direction from where they came. "Good thing one of us is smart." Sam glared at Gabe's back, suddenly wishing he'd let him fall and smack his face against the curb when he gun-butted him. He knew his brother was only kidding and being an ass, but it still pissed him off.

"What do you mean?" Sam ran to catch up to him with Luis on his tail. "When did you put a tracking device on her?" *He touched her?* Maybe he should break a few fingers, too. As far as he was concerned, Jamie Fields was off-limits to any other man. When he looked back at Luis, the old drunk only shrugged.

Gabe released a throaty laugh and shook his head. "Not on *her,* you idiot. On the *briefcase.* Whether she runs off with it or hands it to somebody else, we'll know where it goes, and it's rigged with a little surprise, too." He paused and smirked at Sam. "That's how it's done, brother."

Sam released a deep, pent-up breath. "I'm sorry I hit you with my gun." He felt like an asshole, but not really. Gabe would've done the same to him if Sam was about to pop Mima in the back of the head. "I just couldn't let you shoot her."

Gabe stared at him for a long moment, his brows furrowed and forehead crinkled in frustration, before his eyes widened with awareness. "You fell in love with her, didn't you?"

Luis let out a long whistle. "Oh, boy."

Sam cleared his throat and shifted on his feet. He shrugged, not wanting to admit the truth to these hardened men. One tougher than granite, the other usually drunk. "She's...fun."

"And could get you killed."

"Maybe that's what I deserve."

"Maybe it is."

Silence dragged on as they eyeballed each other. Finally, Gabe checked his watch. "I need a fuckin' drink. How about you?"

"Yes!" Luis answered from the back.

"We should be going after her, not drinking! What the fuck is wrong with you?"

"I'm going for a drink, with or without you. I'm tired of being told I can't have a shot of whiskey until after 5 p.m.," Gabe belted. Sam raised an amused brow, surprised Mima managed to control this brutish bastard. It was actually a funny bit of knowledge he'd have to remember. "And after I finish a good sip and see what's inside this briefcase, I'll check the tracker. Is that quick enough for your lonely pecker?"

No, it isn't. Sam fell in step with Gabe, feeling really low and pissed-off at the same time. He had a nagging feeling that Jamie could be in serious trouble. The boys could think all they want about him living by the eye of his pecker, but that wasn't true. Sure, he'd had his fun, but he wasn't a man-whore. He had a heart and feelings and needs like anybody else in this world. He just didn't show his as much as others, didn't wear his heart on his sleeve. For that, he felt alone. Maybe if he opened up a little more, he'd have something good in his life.

He didn't care about the fucking briefcase. Jamie worried him most. What if the person she was working for decided to beat her up, or even kill her? If they suspected that she knew something, well then there was one sure way of shutting her up.

They made their way to Zamira's. She closed and locked the door behind them for privacy as they opened the briefcase.

As promised, yet to everyone's surprise, everything was there. Video surveillance, photos, voice recordings, even a record book with cash transactions of drug lords from Spain to Canada, and everywhere in between.

"How is this even possible?" Gabe said, his expression wrought with barely suppressed rage and utter shock. "Even I didn't know all of this."

"Got to be somebody who worked with Colton since the beginning," Sam added. "There are men in these photos who are long dead."

Zamira clucked her tongue. "Only Ben was with him from the start, and he's dead, too." She eyeballed Sam and gave a brief nod before she headed toward the back room.

Sam glanced at Gabe who was engrossed in the contents of the briefcase. He slid out of his chair and followed Zamira. He didn't know what she wanted, but Sam was glad to get away from Gabe for a moment or two.

He entered the room as Zamira switched on the overhead lights. "Close the door," she said, and wandered to a shelf along the back wall. As Sam closed the door behind him, Zamira hit a switch and to Sam's amazement, the panel slid to the side, revealing a weapons' stash that could rival that of the deadliest of warlords. He couldn't hide his shock. Some of those guns were worth more than a new vehicle.

Zamira stood there, hands on generous hips, looking up at her collection as a mother might gaze upon her newborn child. "I've been collecting some of these for over thirty years now. Some were given to me, some I took," she giggled, "and some of them are yours."

Sam walked up and admired the collection of pistols, rifles, machine guns, and various knives. He shook his head in bewilderment. He knew Zamira was the right hand to a Cuban kingpin in her younger days, but he had no idea—

"What do you mean some of these are mine?" He stared at her in confusion. They may be friends, but he was pretty certain he played no part in this collection.

Zamira turned around and Sam's eyes bulged at the rare and pristine Persian contract Luger with its long barrel resting in her hands. It was one of only a thousand ever made.

"Do you know where this came from, *mijo*?"

He frowned, staring at the gun as if it was made of pure gold. "No. Should I?"

Her sad smile sunk right into his heart. "This is a gift to you from your mother."

He blinked. "My mother?"

Zamira nodded and lifted her hands, gesturing for Sam to take it. As he held the weight of the rare piece in his hands, he was beyond confused by this odd conversation. A strange conversation that was making his heart pound.

"Rose was instructed not to tell you the truth about your parents. There is a reason why they didn't visit you as much as they should have, my boy. Because it was too dangerous."

He frowned. This wasn't making any sense. His parents were irresponsible party animals that didn't give a shit about him and their responsibilities. Maybe they loved him, in some small way, but they certainly didn't show it.

"Your parents were spies, Samuel. They met on a job and fell in love." The love and pride he saw in her big brown eyes made his breath hitch. "When you came along, they had to make a decision. It was either me or Rose who would take you in, but I wasn't in a position to raise a child."

Sam shook his head. "You or Auntie Rose? I don't understand…"

Zamira smiled and reached her weathered hand up to touch his hair. "Your mother and Rose are my sisters."

"You're my aunt?" Sam couldn't believe it. All along he thought they were just friends, connected to the business. He couldn't hide his shock. "I thought you were Cuban."

She clucked her tongue. "I am. You are, too. Our family is Afro-Cuban, Samuel, and your father's side is Irish, which I'm sure you already knew."

Sam blew out a long, exasperated breath. "This is a lot to take in."

"It's a small world, is it not? I had been doing business with Colton for many years before he took you in. The first time you walked into this place, it took everything in me not to tell you the truth. I stayed because of you, to watch over you. I promised your mother I would."

"Wait a minute. You said my parents *were* spies? What are they doing now? I haven't seen them in"—he had to think hard to the last special occasion when Auntie Rose burned the turkey—"since last Thanksgiving, I think."

Tears filled Zamira's eyes, and after a long silence…he knew. His throat clinched tight. He struggled to breathe. "How? When?" It felt as if the last breath of air parted his lungs, never to be taken again.

She wiped her tears and squared her shoulders. "It was a car accident a week ago. They were together, that's all the detail I know." She cleared her throat and smiled up at him, big brown eyes glistening. "They left everything to you. A villa in Spain. A chalet in Alaska. Even a yacht here on the island, although I must tell you that your Uncle Luis doesn't want to part with it."

He wanted to smash his fist through a window. A week ago his life had begun to change at the same time as his estranged parents took their last breath. Did they think of him as they died together?

"That drunk husband of yours is my uncle, eh?" Sam chuckled and shook his head, trying to make light of the news but numb at the same time. "How did I get so lucky?" He didn't want her to see the depth of his pain.

"You are very lucky to have Luis as your uncle, you silly boy. He'd kill for you."

Overloaded with this information, he turned toward the rack of weapons, his mind filled with the rare moments he saw his parents. Now that he was older and wiser in life, it suddenly dawned on him all those moments when his mother hugged him hard before having to leave again. He hated her then. He regretted not knowing her now. Suddenly, he missed her beautiful face. Her sweet smile. Those dark eyes, almost black, staring at him with what must've been love. He just didn't know it then.

A week ago, as his parents drove to their demise, Sam was heading out to kill a woman that he apparently fell in love with. A woman who might very well be a spy, or at least, the pawn of a blackmailer. He shook his head as his heart ached.

He jerked when Zamira touched his shoulder. Tears had filled his eyes. Why now? Why did they have to die before he could know the truth about them?

"Don't be like them, *mijo*," she whispered. "That's no way to live. You still have years of life and love, and maybe children, ahead of you. If this woman I saw you with is the one you want, then you go after her. Don't let life slip through your fingers as your parents did."

He shook his head, at war with what he should do. "That woman might be the death of me."

Zamira clucked her tongue and released a throaty laugh. "As all women should be, my boy. Otherwise, what fun would life and love be?"

With a groan of anguish, he turned around and gathered Zamira in his arms and hugged her hard. He had no words. Nothing he could ever say would adequately describe the pain in his heart over his parents, the happiness to know that Zamira and Luis were family, or the insecurity of his love for Jamie. What would come of it all?

"I know it's hard, sweetheart." She rubbed his back as Sam let his tears fall unheeded. "You can't be tough forever."

When she stepped back and gazed up at him, Sam knew that this woman he'd cared for, for many years as a dear friend, was tough as nails and smart as a whip. He couldn't be more elated to learn that they shared the same blood.

"Come now," she said, pressing the button to close the paneled wall. They walked arm in arm from the back room. He quickly wiped his tears before the others noticed. Gabe would never let it go if he saw Sam crying. They were men after all. Only women cried.

Gabe looked up from a handful of photos, a quizzical look on his face. Luis sat beside him, and when the old man glanced up and smiled, Sam couldn't help his own. They nodded in silent awareness. One day they would have a good talk, and he would tell Luis that the yacht he suddenly inherited could stay right here. Sam had no use for it anyway.

Gabe looked from Luis to Zamira, to Sam again, and shook his head. "What's with you guys today?"

"I'll tell you later, shitstick," Sam said, his voice thick with emotion. He was anxious to find Jamie. "Check your tracker before I lose my patience. I'm done waiting around for you."

"Still haven't learned anything, have you? Well, you're on your own with that one." Gabe shook his head, pulled his cell phone out of his pocket and checked the location of the briefcase. "It's heading west out of the city. Route 1."

"*Lleva el coche,*" Zamira said to Luis. He raised his brow and chuckled as he slipped out of his chair and disappeared through the door leading into the alley out back.

A few minutes later, Sam heard a rumble out front. He walked up to the windows looking onto the street and laughed out loud as Luis got out of a beat-up Plymouth Belvedere straight out of the fifties.

"Don't let the looks fool you," Zamira commented. "That baby will get you anywhere, and quick."

Sam looked over his shoulder. Gabe sat there shaking his head at him. It was time his brother was put into his place.

"You and Terry got what you wanted. At least give me the chance to find out if I can have mine."

Gabe's top lip twitched as he nodded. The humor in his eyes changed into something more like understanding, and concern. "Want me to come with you for backup?"

Sam shook his head. "Nah. You burn the contents of that briefcase then go home to Mima. Tell Terry I have everything under control. I need to do this alone."

"I'm not leaving until I know you're okay. Argue with me all you want, I'm still four months older than you."

"And not blood related."

"Does that really matter?" Gabe raised his brows high, waiting for the right answer.

A slow smile crossed Sam's face as they eyeballed each other. "No, it doesn't."

"Good. Now fuck off and go after that girl. I'll keep you updated on the location, bud. Be careful."

Sam took one last look at Gabe and Zamira, hoping it wouldn't be his last. He walked through the door and approached Luis who was leaning against the passenger door, a fat cigar hanging from his mouth. A swirl of pungent smoke wafted up in the air above his five-foot frame.

"Are you sure you can handle this beast?"

Sam chuckled, reached out, and shook his hand. "You know it."

"You bring this back in one piece or your aunt will have my balls." He smacked the roof of the car twice then headed toward the bar without looking back.

"I promise." Sam got into the driver's seat and shifted the beast into gear. The old Plymouth sped off toward Route 1, as if old Luis put a Hemi under its rusty hood.

He had a woman to catch.

Chapter 9

After an hour-long stifling drive out of the city, Jamie pulled her rental car up to what appeared to be an abandoned hotel in the middle of nowhere. After making the exchange earlier that day, and the gunfire she'd heard as she'd gotten into her taxi, she decided at the last minute to rent a car.

She thought she'd seen the guy she gave the briefcase to following her, but she couldn't be certain from all the people and traffic condensing the streets. It was too much to take in all at once. She wasn't used to this insanity, she wasn't a female version of James Bond. Somebody had fired a bullet at her. This was real. Very real. But no matter how terrified she felt, she had to be tough and pull through—if not for herself, then at least for Monty.

Vines covered one side of the building. A tree pushed through one of the windows on the other. She imagined the hotel to be a stunning vision in its heyday, but now, after many years left to rot in the ever-changing weather, it was a sad sight to behold.

She stared through the car window, unsure if she wanted to get out of the vehicle. This looked like the perfect place to commit murder. Nobody was around. She could probably scream and nobody would hear her.

This is it. This is the end of the road.

Behind a huge hibiscus bush she noticed a small car sitting there with nobody behind the wheel. If she didn't notice fresh tire tracks behind the car she would've thought the vehicle had been abandoned long ago, just like the hotel. She took a deep breath to regulate the pace of her pounding heart. She had to be tough now. Had to do whatever she could to ensure Monty's safe release. Get this done and over with, and return to some normalcy. Anything was better than this.

Jamie opened the door and stepped out, holding the briefcase tight to her side. She wandered around the side of the building, not sure exactly where she was supposed to meet the contact. She hadn't been told any names, wasn't given any descriptions of faces. She was left completely in the dark on this insane adventure. But she couldn't turn back now, even if she wanted to tuck her tail between her legs and flee.

A lizard scurried from beneath a nearby shrub, making her jump back and suck in a sharp breath. It quickly disappeared beneath the overgrowth of vine climbing up the crumbling façade.

"Hello?" Jamie peered through an old window, long void of glass. Inside the weathered building she noticed what was once beautiful dark wood furniture completely covered in a blanket of dust. Everything was covered in a thick layer of time, which also proved that her contact did not pass through this way. Back in its day this place must have been a beautiful hotel with its high ceilings, numerous columns, lovely archways, and a grand staircase in the middle of the floor. But none of that mattered with so much at stake.

She kept pushing forward, growing more nervous with each passing second and not a response from the person she was supposed to meet. She jerked around and clutched her throat as a huge parrot, followed by a flock of small black birds, flew out of a tree right beside her. She blew out a startled breath. Freaked out and on edge was the understatement of the decade. Now that she thought about it, it seemed that every time she turned around, something jumped out to scare her.

When she took a turn at the back of the building and into an overgrowth of vines and shrubs at the garden, she saw a woman dressed in a black pantsuit, sitting on a low garden wall near the treeline. Stiff and straight, the woman sat poised as if she had royalty running through her veins. Chin high, dark hair pulled back tight, blood red lipstick on her thin lips. Jamie instantly hated her. This woman had the look of a true bitch who was used to getting everything she wanted.

On the ground in front of her kneeled Monty, with his hands tied in front of him.

"Monty!"

Jamie rushed toward him but halted when Monty lifted his bruised face and shook his head. He didn't want her coming too close. Never before had she seen her friend act this quiet, as if he was afraid to speak, afraid to exist.

She stood frozen to the spot as the woman gave her a long, thorough perusal, before she smiled like a fox. For the first time in her life, Jamie wanted to kill somebody. She wanted to wring her neck for putting her and Monty through this hell. She portrayed pure evil from a single glance.

"I have your briefcase, now let Monty go."

The woman lifted her hand and waggled perfectly manicured fingers for Jamie to bring her the case. "After you. Come on, I don't have all day."

Jamie's steps faltered, but she pushed forward. The deed was almost done, and now she could get Monty safely away from here and go home. Back to regular life without all of this bullshit and danger. If she could take back this job, she would. Not only did this woman hurt her only friend, she put Jamie in serious danger. Those two thugs could've hurt or killed her. On top of that she fell in love with a man who probably wasn't what she thought him to be. The hardest part to deal with was not knowing for sure. Even with all that she'd suffered as a child, nothing compared to the heartache of this trip to Cuba.

"Did anyone follow you?"

Jamie lifted her chin. She wasn't going to back away in fear from this woman. "No. I don't think so."

The woman took the case from Jamie's outstretched hand. Greed flashed in her eyes as she set the case down, punched in a code, and opened the lid.

Jamie's eyes widened at the money piled right to the top of the briefcase. There must be a million bucks in that case. *I had that with me for the past three hours? Holy shit.*

The woman looked up with a smile. "Not bad, eh?"

Jamie blinked. "Not bad?" Dread filled her stomach as she glanced down at Monty. He hung his head, but not before she saw the defeat in his eyes. Jamie felt horrible for him. Her friend, who was the life of the party, and the funniest man she knew, had no light left in his eyes. Jamie knew then that Monty was telling the truth when he said he didn't know what was in the briefcase. He, too, was a pawn to this woman, and he probably felt ashamed for getting Jamie caught up in this.

She couldn't help a slight jab at this horrible woman. "You offered me a lousy fifty grand to go to all this trouble, when you probably have over a million in there? You must be pretty fucking cheap."

The woman's head snapped up, eyes wide with affronted shock, before she tilted her head back and cackled like a witch. "A million? Ha! Try ten million, honey."

Ten million. Jamie wouldn't even know what to do with that amount of money.

She must have traded something horrible in order for this woman to get that obscene amount of cash. But Jamie didn't want to know the details.

She wanted no part of it. Knowing too much got people killed—that was a fact of life. Knowing how much she suffered to get this woman all that dirty money, was a hard blow to take.

The woman reached into her suit jacket and withdrew an envelope, handing it to Jamie. "Here's the rest of your money. You've earned it."

Earned it. Jamie took a step back and shook her head. "I don't want it. I don't want any part of this shit. Just let us go."

The woman tipped her head back and laughed again. Jamie hated her with all the passion a damaged woman could feel. Maybe she ruined someone's life for all that money. People could've died. Maybe some did. It made her stomach turn thinking she could be to blame for someone's death.

"Believe me, honey, you should take it. Do you want to know what you exchanged for this money?" She waved the envelope in the air.

Jamie shook her head. "No, I don't. I just want to go home. I'm tired of this game. If I would've known what this was about, I wouldn't have taken the job, for any amount of money."

"Oh, really? Not even to pay off your pimp?"

Jamie glared at her. "What are you talking about? I'm not a hooker." She glanced down at Monty, but his attention was still on the ground in front of him.

"It wasn't from him," the woman said in a haughty tone. "Once I knew your name, I found out everything I needed to know. Just like I know you were behind on rent. You had to take this job."

Jamie blinked hard. "So you had this all set up no matter what I would've said? You made sure I had no choice." She blew out a hard breath and stared out in the distance to nothing in particular. Being used was a hard pill to swallow.

The evil woman smiled. "Of course. I had to make sure."

"You're a fucking bitch."

She grinned like a she-devil. "That briefcase you were carrying held all the secrets to a very dangerous organization, little girl. Secrets about men who would kill you and your family over a kilo of cocaine, or a briefcase with money. My husband and I used to work for them." She closed the lid of the briefcase and stood, leaving Jamie's envelope on the garden wall. Jamie had a hard time not staring at that envelope, knowing what that money could do for her, yet unsure if it was worth it. "Your little lover isn't the man you think he is, nor is his family. This money is to keep my mouth shut about their business dealings. These are very dangerous men you're fucking with."

Jack? An immediate sob wrenched from her throat. *No. Not him.* It felt like she'd gripped Jamie's heart and squeezed her life from it. "How do you know who I was with? Were you following me here, too?"

"I wasn't, but my husband was. He's quite memorable. Big. Bald. Scars on his face."

The man from the hotel. Jamie shuddered, becoming painfully aware that all this time these dangerous people had her in their grip since day one. This woman's husband was right there in the hallway as Jamie left Jack's room the first time. As all of this information began to sink in, Jamie realized she was duped right from the beginning. It wouldn't have mattered what choice she'd made, the path had already been set out for her.

"I had to make sure you got my money, and that you weren't working for the other side."

"Why didn't you just do this on your own? Why involve me, or Monty?" Anger swelled to the surface. "I could've been killed over that stupid briefcase!" Jamie stepped forward and was about to pounce on her, but stopped short when the woman pulled a small handgun from the pocket of her jacket. The click of the hammer pulling back made her face pale. This woman could end her life with one squeeze of that trigger.

"I wouldn't do that if I were you."

"Don't, Jamie. She'll kill you," Monty said, finally paying attention to the exchange.

Jamie stood there with her heart in her throat, and rage boiling in her veins. She was scared, but she was angrier. "Just let us go. Take your money and leave."

The woman started backing away, her gun pointing right at Jamie's chest.

But Jamie needed to know. She had to know the truth about the man she'd fallen in love with. Her voice sounded desperate and husky with emotion. "Tell me about Jack."

"Who's Jack?"

* * * *

Sam skidded to a stop in front of the abandoned hotel. He slammed the car in park and jumped out, running past two cars parked at the side of the building. He barreled around the corner, the prized gun from his mother in hand, and halted at the sight in front of him.

Jamie spun around with tears in her eyes. He knew in that split second that she had discovered the truth. His heart sunk to his stomach.

A man he recognized from the lodge was on his knees with his hands tied in front of him. It became obvious to Sam that the man was Jamie's friend, and that was probably why Jamie ran off on him, because she probably didn't have a choice.

And standing there holding the briefcase was Amanda Cain—Ben's widow.

"Hello, *Sammy*. Did you miss me?"

Her voice made his insides turn to ice. Of all the people he and Gabe thought could be behind this, her name was never mentioned. When Terry took care of Ben after his betrayal, Amanda had disappeared. They all knew she never loved Ben—her heart had always been for Gabe—which was probably why they never suspected her. She was a tough cookie and never one to open her mouth about anything or anyone. Knowing now that she was behind this was a horrible betrayal to all of them.

"Who are you?" Jamie whispered fiercely at Sam. Her big green eyes glistened with tears, yet the anger he saw there nearly brought him to his knees. He never wanted to hurt or betray her, but in the end, as his job often did, people got hurt. He hated himself for that. He deserved to be raked over a chainsaw blade for putting her through this. Sam would take that gladly just to see her smile again.

"Miss Fields, meet Samuel Hayes, one of the deadliest shooters on the planet. Give him twenty grand and he'll kill your father for you. He'd kill your best friend's kid if you paid him enough."

Sam grit his teeth as Amanda's snarky voice raked his nerves. He'd never killed a kid and he never would—no matter the price. But he couldn't take his eyes off of Jamie. The way she looked at him now, as if her whole world just fell apart, ripped his heart out. What could he possibly say to her to make things right? He'd rather be tortured than faced with the challenge of expressing his emotions. Anything was better than standing here without knowing what to do…or what to say in his defense.

"Cat got your tongue?" Amanda purred. "Why don't you tell your little girlfriend why you're here? Why not tell her everything?"

"Jamie, I—"

Her eyes widened. "Watch out!"

Something slammed into his side, taking him down hard. The gun flew out of Sam's hand as he landed hard on the gravel. When he caught his breath, Sam rolled onto his back. His eyes bulged in total shock as a familiar face leaned over him, before a huge fist smashed into his jaw.

Ben.

Sam's head rolled to the side as his mind fought to make sense of what happened. This didn't seem real. How could Ben still be alive? All this time, as business went on and we believed him to be dead, Ben had just been biding his time. Waiting for the right moment to strike. Sam wasn't here when the deed went down but he had heard what happened. When Gabe crashed his plane into the Canadian Rockies and Mima nursed him back to life, Ben had decided to make his move. With a multimillion-dollar stash of cocaine in the belly of that plane, Ben went after him with the intent to get rid of Gabe and cash in on the blow. But Ben didn't expect Terry to be sent in the chopper with him, so Ben pointed his gun at Terry instead. Luckily, with Mima's help, Gabe and Terry managed to stop him, but not before he tortured and nearly killed Mary. For that, Terry strung Ben up, slit his ankle, and lowered him down to the pigs.

Sam knew that Terry could never watch that—not when his mother died of a heart attack when Terry was a boy, because she saw what they did. Terry had lost his real mother because his father had trained those pigs to eat human flesh.

His old mentor reached down, grabbed a handful of Sam's shirt, forcing him to his feet. "I was hoping Terry would've joined you. But I guess that little cunt has more important things to do than your dirty work, eh, Sammy?" Ben balled his fist and slugged him in the nose. "I hear sweet little Mary had a baby girl. I'll have to pay them a visit and bring her some carnations."

Sam stumbled back and groaned as blood gushed over his lips. Ben always did have a mean punch. "Not while I'm alive." He spit out the blood from his mouth and shook away the dizzy heat threatening to take him down again. "I thought you were dead."

Ben laughed loud and hard. "Terry should've waited by the pen to see it through. But we both know he never had the stomach for that. My wife pulled me out just in time."

Sam lifted his fists and dodged to the side as Ben jabbed his knuckles at his face and missed. Sam circled around him, waiting for the right moment to make his attack. His heart pounded and his fists shook with his rage. Ben had been his mentor and his friend. Colton had trusted him. They all did, until Ben tried to kill Terry.

Now Benjamin Cain and his wife were nothing but a waste of breath to Sam. After everything the family had done for them, they were still greedy enough to blackmail them. To Sam, knowing they'd put Jamie at risk enraged him more than anything. His brothers knew how to defend themselves and their families, but Jamie didn't have anybody. She was alone in this world, but if she'd ever forgive Sam, then she wouldn't have to be alone any more.

"Why are you doing this, Ben? You were a part of the family."

As much as Sam didn't want to have to fight back, he knew he had no choice or Ben would kill him, and Jamie, too. He couldn't risk her getting hurt.

"I was never part of your family," he sneered. "I was just the muscle Colton needed. You boys were the family. You have no idea how much I hated and envied you."

Jealousy could turn a good man into a crazy fool. As Sam stared into Ben's eyes, he knew the old Ben was long gone. As Ben limped forward, Sam's gaze halted on his gun five feet away. He needed to get his hands on it because he knew he was no match for his mentor. Even though those pigs had done a number on his legs, Ben was still a strong man full of rage, hatred, and jealousy.

Sam sidestepped as Ben rushed him and dove for his gun. The big guy was on him in a flash. They rolled in the dirt, fighting for the upper hand. The gun was only inches from his reach, but every time his fingers brushed the handle, Ben hit him again, and again. He could barely see through his right eye as blood trickled down from his eyebrow.

"Hurry up and kill him!"

Distracted by the shout, Ben jerked around and looked at his wife. Sam gave him a left hook which stunned the big man enough for Sam to shove him away. He flipped over and reached for the gun, but not quickly enough for Ben to be on him again. His big hands grabbed Sam's neck from behind and squeezed.

Sam's eyes bulged from the force of Ben's grip. He fought to control his breathing, knowing he had a minute or less before he'd take his last breath and it would be over.

"Jack!" Jamie cried.

"Stay back," Amanda warned.

Sam grit his teeth. He had to fight this. He couldn't give up. Not now. Not when Jamie's life was in his hands. With Ben's three-hundred pounds of insanity on his back, choking the life from him, Sam gathered every ounce of strength he had and pushed up on his elbows and knees with Ben still on him. Every vein in his face threatened to burst as he pushed up from the ground, his legs shaking, his lungs almost finished. With a growl of pure rage and dwindled strength, Sam dug his fingers into Ben's forearms, bent forward, and threw Ben off his back.

As Ben hit the dirt, Sam shouted, "Run!" at Jamie, before Ben jumped up and dove for his midsection.

Sam raised his knee and got Ben hard in the groin. As the big guy groaned and slunk to his knees, Sam reached for his gun.

A shot cracked the air. A woman screamed.

As Ben reached out to wrestle the gun away from him, Sam pulled the trigger. The loud bang echoed over the scene as the side of Ben's head blew open. Blood and brains spattered the bushes beside them.

Sam exhaled and dropped down on the dirt beside Ben's body. He cringed in pain as he wiped the blood from his swollen eye and his cut mouth. Exhaustion barely grazed the surface of how he felt. He sucked in a deep breath and exhaled. It felt as if his chest wanted to cave in from throwing Ben's huge body off of him.

That's when he heard her crying. He pushed up to his knees and looked toward the garden wall.

There, holding the other man's limp body was Jamie.

A vehicle revved up and took off down the road.

Amanda was gone. But that wasn't what had Sam's full attention. It was how tightly Jamie had that man in her arms, and how she cried for him as if she loved him. Sam wanted her to love him like that. To be afraid for his life. To cry over him.

Jamie's sobbing reached right into his chest and sliced his heart to pieces. She rocked back and forth holding her friend's body as she rubbed his hair away from his ashen face. Her hand shook as she whispered to him, "I'm so sorry, Monty. I'm so sorry. I tried to do everything. I tried to save us."

Monty's eyes fluttered open and he said something to Jamie that Sam couldn't hear. His eyes then closed again and his head rolled to the side.

Sam pushed up to his feet and went to her. All the pain in his body was nothing compared to the vision of her holding her friend's body. When she glared up at Sam with tears rolling down her cheeks, he knew he'd lost her.

"He took a bullet for me," she cried, having no idea that Sam would do the same. He'd do the same every goddamned day. "He was just trying to help me! Why? Who are these people?"

"I'm sorry." Sam closed his eyes and hated himself for not knowing what else to say. He wanted to hold her and protect her and show her that he wasn't the demon she thought him to be. If he could take everything back, he would. He'd go right back to the lodge, to that night on the dock, and he would've stayed there with her. He enjoyed being there for that short time. The peace he felt there could never be replaced anywhere else. But if he were to be honest with himself, he'd feel at peace where she was, wherever that would be. Home isn't a place, it's where the heart is.

He'd kill for her. That's all he knew how to do.

Jamie gently laid Monty back down and stood. She stared down at him for a long while before she looked back at Sam. "I wanted to trust you. I was going to tell you everything when you came out of the shower this morning, and then that woman called."

"I—"

"But then you turned out to be a fraud anyway! You kill people for a living?" She choked on her last words, and stared past him to Ben's body. She shuddered. "I don't even know you." The terror and rage in her eyes made Sam shut his mouth. "This whole trip you badgered me with questions, when all along, I was just a delivery girl and you were the one sent to entrap me and kill me! What kind of man are y-you?"

Sam exhaled in defeat. He had no argument, because she was right. Maybe he was a monster. Maybe he should slink away in the shadows never to return again. He deserved that lonely fate.

"Everything you said…was a lie."

Her shoulders shook as she hung her head and quietly cried. He couldn't help himself—despite her hatred of him. Sam walked up to her and put his arms around her. Her arms hung at her sides, her body trembled, as he held her tight in his arms.

His heart pounded when he realized that this would be the last time he saw her, got to hold her, got to hear her voice and look at her beautiful face.

"I didn't want to do it," he murmured, his voice clipped. "I took the job not realizing that I'd fall in love you."

She pulled back and stared up at him, her mouth open in shock.

"I think I fell in love with you that night on the dock." He let out a deep sigh, trying to find the right words as she stood there, trembling. "When I saw you on the terrace on your first day here, I didn't want it to be you. And if I could take it all back, I would."

She stared up at him, eyes wide and wet with tears, but she said nothing.

"I've been alone most of my life, Jamie. Until recently I never really knew my family. The men I work for, and with, have been there for me, and I don't deny that I've done some terrible things. But I'm not a monster. I had to protect them, that's why I took this job."

He set her at arm's length, even though he didn't want to. "I think it's best if you go home now. Put this place behind you."

Her chin quivered. "What about Monty?"

"I'll make sure he gets home. I promise."

"What are you going to do?" Tears rolled down her cheeks and it made his own eyes burn with despair.

"I'm going to finish what I started."

As the woman he loved walked toward the abandoned building, she paused at the corner and looked back at him. The sadness and longing he saw in her eyes made him want to sink to his knees and scream to the blue sky. Life wasn't fair and love was painful. Why didn't Gabe and Terry warn him how horrible this feeling would be?

A vision of his mother smiling at him made his heart ache even more. As much as he hated how they left him, it made him wonder if his choices in life were just a version of theirs. His mother was beautiful, with dark eyes, perfect brown skin, and teased hair just like Auntie Rose. She could've been a model, could've been anything. But she chose his crazy Irish father instead, with the horrible blond mustache and tall, white, gangly body. They were the complete opposite, but they fell in love hard. That much Sam knew. He recalled how they looked at each other during their rare visits with such heartache and fear and longing it was gross for a kid to look at. But now that Sam was a grown man, he knew what that meant. They were afraid to lose each other. To him, that was real love. Real passion. Real life.

He was afraid of losing Jamie, but he still had to finish his job.

When Jamie disappeared around the corner, Sam took a deep breath and made his way over to her friend's body to check his wound, all the while thinking about the love his parents had for each other, right until their deaths. If only he could be luckily enough to have that one day.

The bullet got Monty just below the shoulder. It wasn't life threatening. His pulse was weak but it was there.

As he heard Jamie drive away, Sam pulled out his cell phone and dialed Gabe who answered immediately.

"So?"

"I need you to set that trigger."

Twenty seconds later a bomb exploded in the distance. He'd never felt such relief before in his life. He glanced over at Ben's body, to the pool of blood soaking into the ground. Ben deserved to be left there for the animals to finish.

Sam picked Monty off the ground and carried him to Zamira's car to gently lay him across the back seat. If this man was a friend of Jamie's, then he'd take good care of him. Then he returned to the garden wall and grabbed the envelope for Jamie. She may not want it, but he'd make sure she got it somehow. It was clear to him that she took this job delivering the briefcase because she had to. She did it for the money.

He returned to the car and looked back to see Monty's eyelids fluttering. He'd be okay, as long as Sam got him to a hospital by nightfall.

He barreled down the dirt road toward the main highway and the black smoke curling up into the sky. There, in the middle of the road, was Amanda's charred body, still clinging to what was left of the steering wheel, as tiny pieces of ten million bucks lay scattered all around her. *What a waste. All that money.*

He shook his head in disbelief, grabbed his cell, and punched in Terry's number. His brother answered on the third ring. "Hey, buddy."

"Hey yourself." He exhaled hard. "It's done."

There was a short pause before Sam heard Terry's sigh of relief. "Who was the woman? Wait. Let me guess. My stepmother?"

"No. I don't think we have to worry about her. Antonio will keep her on a tight leash. Besides, they don't need your money. They're worth ten times what you are."

"True." Terry chuckled. "Who was it, then?"

Sam could tell him that it was Ben all along, with Amanda's help, but he wouldn't. Terry thought he'd killed him. Sam didn't want his brother to feel like he'd failed. "It was one of my rivals, Terry. Nobody you knew."

"Are you okay?"

He almost shed a tear from the expression of defeat on Jamie's face before she walked away. "I'll be all right."

"And the girl?"

"What girl?"

Terry laughed and the baby started crying in the background. Sam winced from the hair-raising scream, then smiled as Terry shushed the baby quiet. He was a good father and Sam was envious. "The one you couldn't keep your hands off of. Gabe told me all about her. Apparently you finally found a normal one."

And I failed to keep her. "Maybe I don't deserve normal."

"I think you do. Don't put yourself down, Sam. You're one of best men I know. Now that this is over you should come home and we'll all have a nice dinner. You'll get your ten million, and then you can go find your girl. I trust you know where she went?"

"I put a tracking device on her back when I kissed her."

Terry chuckled. "You're such a romantic."

Sam frowned when it suddenly struck him. "*My* ten million? What are you talking about?"

"That's your payoff and your retirement for doing this last job, brother. I think it's time you grow up like the rest of us. Did you really think I had that briefcase filled with real money? We have crooked friends for a reason, you know."

Sam couldn't help his incredulous laughter. "I should've known. Does Gabe know my retirement is larger than his?"

"That'll be between you and me," Terry murmured into the phone.

Sam smiled. It felt good having one up on Gabe for a change. "I'll be home soon."

As Sam and an unconscious Monty headed back to Havana, he imagined what life would be like now that it was over. Quiet days and nights ahead. No more looking over his shoulder. No more screaming—except from his brothers' babies.

He knew he'd never be good enough for Jamie. She deserved everything good in the world. A good, gentle man who'd spoil her rotten and exhaust himself keeping her happy. A man who would touch her with a gentle hand by day, and ravish her rough at night, with everything in between of course. He wanted to give her some of those screaming babies, too, even if it meant giving it to her every single night and day. Which was why he'd never let her walk away that easily.

Even if he had to chase her down for the rest of his days.

Epilogue

The offer to return to Sharp Ridge Lodge couldn't have come sooner. Jamie stared out the window of the twin Otter, her mind lost with the rain pelting the airplane windows.

She had packed her things and left her apartment for good. When the season was over, she planned to move elsewhere. Somewhere new. Somewhere she could start fresh. Definitely nowhere tropical.

The past eight months since leaving Cuba and her insane mission that nearly got her killed, she couldn't wait for the solitude of the bush. A new corporation had bought the lodge from Valerie and, just as Valerie had promised, all staff were invited back to work.

"I wonder what he's doing right now, maybe chasing somebody on a skidoo in the Swiss Alps."

Jamie shook her head and glared at Monty sitting beside her.

Monty had returned from Cuba cleaned up and in excellent health with a scar from a bullet to brag about. He was a changed man, and he couldn't stop talking about Sam as if he was some kind of hero. It made her loneliness even worse. She missed him so bad she hadn't slept a whole night since she'd left his hotel room that fateful morning.

Eight months of sleepless nights and terrifying nightmares when she did manage to catch a wink. "I should've let that woman kill you," she teased. Knowing that Jack—or Sam—had taken good care of him made her miss him dreadfully.

"He carried me into that hospital, Jamie, and he stayed with me until I woke up."

She rolled her eyes and stared out the window. "I know, Monty." Her heart ached as his face came to mind. She'd never feel the soft curls of his thick hair as she feathered her fingers through. Never again would she see the urgent need in his eyes as he looked down at her before pressing his lips to hers. Hot tears rushed to the surface as his gold-toothed grin flashed before her tired eyes. Why did he have to be so wonderful? Killer or not, she just wanted to see him and hold him again. She wanted to feel his strength wrapped around her. That was all that really mattered. She wasn't perfect either. Nobody was in this crazy world.

"Why don't you call him?"

As the twin Otter soared over the endless wilderness of the north, closer to the place where she'd first met him, a nervous ball filled her stomach. "I can't. We live two very different lives."

"He's just a regular guy—"

"Who happens to kill people," she snapped. Her eyes widened as Monty's face lowered and his brows slanted with a frown. "I'm sorry. You didn't deserve that. I'm just…frustrated."

Monty nodded. The poor guy had had to deal with her shitty attitude for eight months now, but like a great friend, he took it in stride. "If you never found out that part of his life, would you be with him?"

Jamie stared out the window and tucked a loose strand of hair behind her ear, thinking about his question. "Maybe." But Jamie knew she'd figure out Sam's secret eventually, and then she'd grow to resent him for lying to her. She believed that when a person loved somebody, they should never lie to them, and they certainly shouldn't lie about where their income is coming from. They shouldn't tell their girlfriend that they just landed a new account at a firm when really, they got paid to shoot a man in the back of the head. That's quite a big difference. One could mean climbing the corporate ladder and becoming successful, the other could mean walking into a six-foot cell and never seeing their loved ones in private ever again. Or death.

But she had to admit, knowing that he was a dangerous man, yet he touched her with such gentleness, with such raw passion, was a turn-on. Sometimes she dreamed about him chasing down an evil villain and then making love to her with his handgun sitting on the bedside table.

Even though she tried not to think about him, every single day she wondered what Sam was doing. She had fallen in love with a hitman. A man who was supposed to kill her but didn't. He wasn't a monster. Monsters don't help their lover's friends. Sam could've left Monty there to die, but he didn't. He could've had somebody else kill her, but he didn't. He told her to get away from there and to put that place behind her. He'd saved her, too. Maybe Monty was right calling him a hero. Still, she was confused and afraid. She couldn't put that place behind her, and she couldn't put him behind her, either.

Jack Daniels and Sam Hayes broke down that wall she had erected long ago. As much as she wanted to run to him and figure out a way to be together and to be safe, she feared that he could get hurt or killed over of her, because she knew he would protect her at all costs, even if it meant giving up his own life.

A man like Sam needed danger and excitement, and she couldn't live wondering and worrying if he would make it back home every night. If they were to be together, then he would have to give it up. She couldn't live in constant fear. And if he couldn't handle that, he couldn't have her.

"He told me some things while I was lying there in the hospital."

She blew out a defeated breath and stared out the window, not really listening to him. "I know, Monty. You told me this before."

"But I didn't tell you everything because you were too angry back then."

She closed her eyes and shook her head. Maybe it was time for her to listen to Monty for a change, instead of the other way around. "Okay. What did he say?" She tried to sound interested but failed miserably.

"He said he'd never been in love before."

"Huh." *Neither have I. Look what falling in love does to you.*

"He said he'd never met a woman quite like you before."

"I see." She sighed, and stared hard at an abandoned beaver house in a swamp down below. *If he'd never met a woman like me before, then why did he let me leave?*

"Apparently, Valerie really took him to the cleaners for—"

She jerked around in her seat and glared at him. "For what?"

Monty shrugged, but the sly grin on his freshly shaven face belied his nonchalance as he lounged back in his seat, avoiding her probing stare. Jamie settled back, stiff and uncomfortable by the odd exchange, and stared out the window again, wondering what the hell he meant by that. What did Valerie have to do with anything?

An hour later the Otter circled over the lodge for a rough landing on the choppy water. As the plane taxied toward the dock, Jamie was happy to see old Groundskeeper Jobe was still alive and standing on the second tier of the dock, waiting for them.

"There's your lover," Monty said.

"That's gross. I'm not that desperate." She cringed picturing his liver-spotted hands reaching out for her.

"I'm not talking about Jobe."

Jamie whipped her head around so fast that her neck nearly cracked. She shoved Monty back in his seat to look out the window on the other side of the plane. Beside ol' Jobe stood another man. Her heart pounded a jagged rhythm as hope and happiness made her breath hitch, but she fought away the tears rushing up.

The pilot hopped out of the cockpit and opened the back side door. It felt as though Jamie floated out of that plane as she stepped onto the dock and faced him.

Sam stood there, dressed in khakis and a T-shirt, looking nothing like a hitman or a criminal or anything other than a regular, handsome man who belonged in the bush. His gold-toothed smirk made her stomach flutter with anxiety and passion.

Something was wrong with the air as she sucked in a sharp breath.

"What are you doing here?" she said, trying to hide her excitement. She didn't want him to know how much she missed him and needed him, nearly went insane thinking about him.

"Getting the lay of the land before work starts tomorrow." His hot gaze took her in from hiking boots to baseball cap, before he smiled. "You look fantastic."

Her insides melted a little. How she missed that handsome smile and the sexy view of his killer body. Then she realized what he'd said first. "Working on what?"

"Whatever you tell him to do, twit," Monty added as he walked past her. The two men shook hands, then Monty glanced back with a killer grin. "You're the new boss lady."

Jamie's jaw dropped as everyone left them alone on the dock. "I don't understand…."

"I bought this place because I fell in love with it. And I fell in love with the housekeeper right in this spot under a moonlit night."

Sam walked toward her, and for the life of her, Jamie couldn't move. "I'd like to start from the beginning, if you'd let me." He reached his hand out. "I'm Sam Hayes."

Jamie looked down at his hand as tears welled in her eyes. Seeing him again after eight long months was too much to handle. She put her trembling hand in his as tears rolled down her cheeks.

Right at that convenient moment the rusty hinges screamed in protest as the lodge door opened wide. Otis Redding's "Love Man" blared over the lawn just for a brief moment as a beautiful, older woman with green-rimmed glasses and a perfect afro headed toward a lounge chair. She walked with the air of confidence yet with an easy sway that Jamie immediately liked.

In one hand the woman held a ball of yarn and in the other, she gripped a crochet hook.

Jamie frowned at the strange coincidence over the book she was ordered to carry in Cuba, and seeing this woman carrying that very thing. "Who is that?" she asked, still staring at the woman.

Sam chuckled. "That's my Auntie Rose. I promise you'll love her. Everyone does. She's just visiting for a week then heading to Spain. Maybe Alaska after that."

Jamie glanced back at him in surprise. "Spain then Alaska? Wow, that's quite the vacation."

"One day, if you'd let me, I'll take you there, too. I'll take you wherever you want to go."

No book, no song, no movie could describe the swell of happiness and love she felt in that moment. And relief. For once in her life, Jamie wasn't afraid or nervous of what tomorrow would bring. She swallowed hard, imagining all the wonderful and exciting things they could do together. But first...she looked up at him, trying to blink away her blinding tears. "And your next job, when do you leave for that?"

His crooked grin was already the answer she needed, but he replied, "What job, when I have all this?" He swept his hands out indicating the lodge, and then cupped his warm hands on her cheeks and pulled her in for a hair-raising kiss.

His scent made her dizzy with lust. The intoxicating rush of his lips against hers made her body yearn to be taken by him, and only him. Eight months was a long damn time to wait.

She didn't feel alone anymore, and she didn't care what Jack Daniels did before. What mattered was that Sam Hayes came after her.

Jamie pushed up on tiptoes and whispered, "I'll tell you a secret." She kissed below his ear. "I love you, too."

And this time, she brought him to *her* room.

Don't miss another great Lyrical Press title.

Dirty Deeds

An Eye for an Eye

As owner of Dirty Deeds, a tech-savvy company specializing in the age-old art of revenge, Eden Smith knows first-hand that secrecy is critical. But when a dead body washes up on the shores of Lake Michigan clutching her business card, Eden's well-constructed world begins to fall apart. Apparently, she's not the only one with a passion for payback, and staying alive to outsmart a killer has become her most important job of all.

A Game for a Game

Hardened homicide detective Kelly Riordan is convinced Eden Smith is hiding more than she's willing to admit. Years on the force have taught him that nothing is what it seems, and that couldn't be truer than when it comes to investigating the alluring owner of a revenge-for-hire business. But revealing her past could put everything Eden has worked for in jeopardy. And trusting a man like Riordan goes against the very instincts that have kept her alive this long.

Chapter 1

The office door flew open, and Eden froze at her desk, her gloved hand poised with the syringe in mid-air. Shifting her eyes left, she scanned the frustrated scowl creasing Tanner's pretty face. *Well, shit.*

"I couldn't get past his receptionist. I swear the woman's a member of the KGB." Tanner tore the straw hat off her head, scrunching the rolled brim in her fist. The door hissed closed at her back and the automatic bolt snapped in place. "The guy must've walked past me three times and it was like I didn't even exist."

Dammit. Eden refocused on the chocolate-covered cherry in her fingers and depressed the plunger, filling the candy with exactly one ounce of a powerful liquid laxative. She should've known better. Of all the dumb things Eden had ever done, scheduling herself to be out of the office at the same time Tanner was prepping for her first assignment had to top the charts.

Revenge was a tricky business. Booming, but tricky. And she should've been here to reconfirm the details with Tanner before sending their newest recruit through that door.

"It's those god-awful boots." Mocha looked up from the papers strewn across his desk, his neon orange press-on nails streaking through the fluorescent light as he waved off Tanner's failure. "I told that girl they're too manly, but she wouldn't listen."

Yep, Mocha was right. Eden arched a brow at the tan, ankle-high work boots laced up Tanner's feet. Those clodhoppers belonged in a construction zone, and threw the rest of Tanner's angelic, fresh-off-the-farm attire completely out of whack.

The brown papers rustled against Eden's rubber gloves as she returned the chocolate to the box and selected another cherry. "Did you get made?"

Not that it mattered. This early in the game, it wasn't like getting recognized was the end of the world…even though it could be to Tanner. Balancing her elbow on her blotter, Eden shook an auburn coil out of her eyes and carefully injected the last of the laxative into the center. Those first few trips out were crucial, and Tanner's confidence would play a big part in whether or not she was successful in the future.

"No, I didn't get made." She clomped around the metal desk on Eden's left, dropping her basket of sandwiches on the floor. "Fat chance of that happening if I can't even get past the front gate."

She tossed the hat onto her desk and it skidded over the top like a downed Frisbee, the wide blue ribbon snagging on the edge. Her paisley print skirt puffed from her legs as she plopped onto her chair. Leaning forward to tug at her laces, she tossed a long blonde curl over her shoulder, toeing off her boots and kicking them aside. "I don't know how in the hell you always make this look so easy."

God, Eden remembered those days. She set the needle aside and carefully placed the chocolate in its little nest, centered the padded white sheet inside the box and lowered the lid. How irritating it could be when a scheme fell apart before she even got it up and running. "Try not to get too discouraged, sweetie. Things could be worse."

Easing the chocolates into a sleeve of shrink wrap, she spun her chair toward the machine on the back credenza. A flick of the switch and the conveyer belt hummed. She fed the box through the slot and waited for it to appear on the other side. "If he noticed you, we'd have to start from scratch. At least now we know what doesn't work."

Grant Dufferman's soon-to-be ex-wife had described him as a womanizer. A guy who got his rocks off preying on young women who were shy, naive. Innocents ripe for the picking and in need of some rescuing. Preferably by him.

Tanner's huge blue eyes and healthy Midwestern vibe should've done the trick. The creep was pretty twisted, though. Remove his Ivy League education and six-figure income, and instead of getting caught in bed with the underage daughter of his wife's best friend, Dufferman's sociopathic tendencies would've made him the perfect internet predator.

That being the case, he was also a lot smarter than she'd given him credit for. Eden pursed her lips. And he knew how to play it safe. Apparently, Grant Dufferman had gone the extra mile by surrounding himself with a dedicated staff, which meant getting the information they were after might be tougher than she'd originally anticipated.

"Did you smile? I told you not to smile." The phone rang and Mocha plucked it from the base. "Password." His high-glossed lips curled in a sneer before he dropped the receiver back into the cradle. "Wrong answer, Chuck. Can I get another contestant?"

Eden huffed a laugh, swinging the shrink-wrapped box around to her desk. She tied a wide gold bow around the center, slipped the gift card under the ribbon and snapped off her rubber gloves.

The password system was old school but effective, and ensured them a loyal, referral-based clientele. Those who preferred their dirty little secrets stayed that way. It never ceased to amaze her how much some people would pay to settle a score, and for those who couldn't afford their fee, a trade for services rendered was always negotiable. A girl could never have too many friends in her line of work.

Tugging open her side desk drawer, she pulled out Dufferman's file to take another pass over the information his wife had provided during her interview. Maybe there'd be a useful tidbit in his profile. Something Mocha had found during his research phase so they could be confident right off the top their work wasn't based on a bunch of false accusations.

The front end contained the usual—high-profile job, Mercedes-Benz, weekend squash game with the boys. Boring. Eden flipped the page and kept reading, bumping the chocolate aside with her elbow so she could spread the file open on her desk. Ah ha. She ran her finger along a line of Paris Dufferman's loopy scrawl. Right, right, here was something they might be able to exploit. Coupled with the dozen or so teenage girls he'd used up and tossed aside, seemed as if Dufferman's favorite pastime was loading up on gin and using his fists in the bedroom.

"You need to act nervous, hon. Unsure of yourself. Get his attention while acting like you don't *want* his attention." Standing behind his desk, Mocha shimmied his black spandex mini-skirt down his thighs, the ruffled lapels of his cropped black blazer and orange vee neckline framing his generous cleavage. "And lose the boots. No man in his right mind would go after a delivery girl wearing those steel-toed nightmares. They scream toe jam and bunions."

Eden lifted a photo of Paris from the file, the woman's left eye a hellacious black-and-blue mess, her bottom lip bloody and swollen. Yep. Disgust twisted Eden's stomach and her nostrils flared. Dufferman was one sick puppy, all right. She flipped the picture to find another showing a series of bruises running down Mrs. Dufferman's back. The woman had been right to come to them. This case deserved special attention. The kind Paris had said she hoped to avoid given her status as one of Chicago's premiere socialites. The kind Eden's team specialized in so Mrs. Dufferman would be left clear of any blame.

Mocha's size twelve, patent-leather stilettos left little depression marks in the gray carpet squares as he approached Tanner's desk and plucked the sandwiches off the floor. "Which ones are safe?"

"None of them." Tanner swept the blonde wig off her head, removed her net cap and tossed it beside the straw hat. "Unless you're itching for a bionic case of food poisoning."

He arched a finely tweezed eyebrow and batted his false eyelashes by way of a droll response. Hosiery swishing, he walked the basket past Eden's desk to the door of an adjoining office she'd had converted into a refrigerated room and industrial grade freezer. After he'd tapped the code into the keypad, the bolt slid open with a clunk, and he and the basket disappeared inside.

Eden flipped the file closed. "Did you get anything?"

"Hell, no." Tanner combed her fingers through her dark angular bob, twirled her chair around and fitted the wig on the empty mannequin head sitting on a recessed shelf built into the wall. "I stood there like an idiot until his receptionist finally gave me the stink eye."

Hmmm... Perhaps the time had come to ramp up their efforts. It was imperative Tanner position herself as Dufferman's next, ideal candidate if they hoped to take him down.

Leaning back in her chair, Eden slid open the lower panel on the credenza and lifted out a thick, three-ring binder. "The next time you go in, I'm sending you as Cherry." She set the binder on her desk and paged to the section marked *Virgins*. "She's innocent, but sexy. Has a little more of a wild streak to her than Coral."

Eden tapped the Polaroid Mocha had snapped of her in a soft-pink lace dress, cap sleeves tied with silk ribbon, handkerchief hemline landing a smidge above the knee. The blonde ringlets of the wig added to the baby doll image, but the matching pink pumps made the look classy. Eye-catching, but not ostentatious. She chewed her bottom lip. With the right accessories, Cherry should work nicely. "What time's his lunch?"

Tanner tipped her head back as if Dufferman's schedule was written on the ceiling tiles. "He rides elevator eighteen up from the lower level gym and arrives at his floor anywhere between three minutes after one and one-twelve, depending on how many secretaries cross his path."

Eden smiled and stood, smoothing away the creases in her white linen dress, and curled her finger for Tanner to follow as she walked the narrow lane between the row of desks to the supply room.

While emotional attachments weren't really her thing, Eden had to admit Tanner had found a way into her heart. She reminded Eden of a younger version of herself. A blank slate—no close friends, family scattered across the globe, and too sharp to get stuck inside a cubicle only to dream of a better life.

Tanner was a lost soul who'd fallen through the cracks in the system, just like Mocha and exactly the same as Eden had been before Malcolm had found her and offered her a way out by grooming her to take over the business.

She punched the code into the keypad and led Tanner into the large walk-in closet. Training another to follow in her footsteps was only the first phase in Eden's long-term goals. Goals she'd put on hold far too long, waiting for the day her financial status made them viable.

Another year, maybe two, and she'd finally be able to see them through.

"Here." She lifted the lace dress from Cherry's section on the hanger bar and dropped it on the hook near the three-way mirror, brought over the shoes and set them on the floor. "The next time you go in, I want you to arrive so you and Dufferman end up on the same elevator." Eden pointed for Tanner to stand in the middle of the mirrors, unhooked the dress and held it in front of Tanner's shoulders. "As you're getting off on his floor, trip and drop the basket."

Eden shook the hanger and Tanner squinted, grabbing the dress from Eden's hand. "What if he doesn't stop to help me pick up the mess?"

Plucking Cherry's wig from the mannequin head, Eden brought it over and tugged it down Tanner's dark hair. "Please. The man has a reputation to uphold and you'll be a damsel in distress. He'll not only help you, he'll get you past his receptionist by inviting you into his office. You know. Just to make sure you're okay."

Grasping Tanner's upper arms, Eden leaned close. As much as Tanner had proven she could handle the job, the last thing Eden wanted was Tanner getting hurt. They needed to be careful. Play it every bit as safe. "No matter how much he insists you stay, you get in, sell him the sandwich and get out. The man is dangerous, Tanner. Underestimating him would be a bad mistake. Your only goal at this point is to leave a lasting impression." She tipped her head. "For next time."

Tanner frowned. "And the food poisoning?"

An evil smile curled Eden's lips in the mirror. "Oh, that's just a bonus. By the time we're done with him, a few days in the bathroom will be the least of Grant Dufferman's problems."

* * * *

Flipping up the collar on his leather jacket, Detective Kelly Riordan shot a glance at the icy rain spitting against the windshield of his Dodge Charger before shoving open the door. A freezing blast of wind careened in off the lake, and he winced as a sheet of hard drizzle doused his face.

Mother Nature during October in Chicago could be one mean bitch. He slammed the door and assessed the small group of onlookers standing a few feet down the beach. The flashing lights of the parked squads bounced off their umbrellas, tinting the rainy sheen blue then red.

Well, at least he could count himself lucky the shitty weather had cut down on the rubberneckers. Whatever evidence the rain hadn't washed away, the rest of the scene should be fairly clean.

He swiveled his shoulders to scan the row of stately manors facing the lake. Too bad he hadn't caught the same break with location. A dead body washed up on the shores of this gated Gold Coast community was gonna cause him hell. The DA would be on his ass like white on rice until he'd closed the case.

He swung back toward the beach and jerked his chin at Néna Ramirez as the officer trudged up from the cordoned off area near the water, tossing her long, dark braid over her shoulder. "Whadda we got?"

"Caucasian female, mid-to-late twenties." She stepped onto the black top and stomped her feet, knocking clods of wet sand off her boots. "Working girl, from the looks of her."

Christ, a prostitute. In this area. A headache bloomed behind Kelly's eyes. Fucking great.

"It gets better." Lifting the back of her hand, Ramirez swept a raindrop off the end of her nose, and then nodded toward a middle-aged couple huddled together under a blue umbrella a foot or so from the crowd. "Mr. and Mrs. Weaver. They found the body about an hour ago and called it in. DeFranco's ruled it homicide. Victim took multiple stab wounds to the chest and torso before getting tossed in the lake."

Jesus. Kelly shifted his attention to the medical examiner, squatting over the body, and raked a dripping piece of hair off his brow. "Any ID?"

"No personal effects." Ramirez turned to follow Kelly's stare down toward the scene. "Time of death is still up for grabs, but DeFranco's estimating three days based on water temp and rate of decomp." Pivoting back toward Kelly, she lifted a brow. "He wants her back at the lab before confirming anything."

Yep, that matched square with DeFranco's MO. His Type A personality brought obsessive-compulsive disorder to a whole new level. Hell, if not for his coke-bottle glasses and missing pointy ears, the guy would make the perfect stand-in for Mr. Spock.

Good news was, DeFranco's practice of trusting science over supposition made him the best damn medical examiner in the city, and Kelly trusted his guesstimate over scientific fact any day. He'd been lucky to pull DeFranco on the case.

He nodded and jerked his thumb at the unlucky folks who'd found the victim. "Put 'em in a squad and get 'em some coffee." Doing so wouldn't help. No amount of time or money could scrub the image of a violent murder from a person's brain, especially when it came to the bloated remains of a floater. But at least they'd be warm, tucked out sight for when the local television jackals arrived. "Keep the press clear. I won't be long."

She dipped her chin and walked off as he started down the beach.

Thunder rumbled in the distance. Another wall of icy water hit his face, and Kelly yanked his jacket zipper higher as he ducked under the yellow police tape stationed around the scene. A black plastic tarp covered most of the body—no doubt DeFranco's attempt to keep any more evidence from disappearing—and Kelly couldn't help but razz the guy. Just to make him a little crazier than he already was. "Beautiful weather we're having."

The medical examiner glanced up from where he was bagging the victim's hands and used the edge of his shoulder to shove his glasses back up his nose. "Damn rain makes everything harder."

Tugging a rubber glove from his pocket, Kelly dropped to his haunches and flipped the tarp away from the victim's face.

Shit. He lowered his chin to his chest, one hand hanging limp between his knees. The bright-red dye job, those huge brown eyes staring off into space…

Someone up there really hated his guts. This case just kept getting better and better.

"You know her?"

Kelly nodded. "Street name's Ruby Slipper. She was one of Delroy's girls." Up until a little over a year ago, when the pimp had harassed the wrong John and gotten himself shot in the face. Another peek at the jagged wounds riddling Ruby's body, and Kelly resettled the tarp. This wasn't some drug deal gone bad. A death this brutal had rage murder written all over it. "Archer's gonna be pissed."

Of the two dozen or so girls in Delroy's stable, Ruby had been the only one to take the asshole's death for the blessing it'd been. While most of his prostitutes had shifted their regulars to other pimps, gone solo or disappeared altogether, Ruby had done the unthinkable and approached Archer for help. Being the stand-up guy he was, he'd agreed to her proposition, leveraging his status as Chicago's lead narcotics detective by making sure she had a roof over her head and money to live on in exchange for information. Valuable information.

The two of them had worked well together. Thanks to Ruby's tips, Archer had made several big busts over the past few months. Hell, he'd even called Kelly in to assist on a few of the arrests.

Telling Archer Ruby was their latest floater was gonna suck, but better he hear it from Kelly than anyone else. If such a thing as best friends existed, they were it. Besides, Archer would need Kelly's okay to get involved in the case. Something he was bound to insist upon.

DeFranco's CSI team wheeled a gurney over the sand and Kelly stood, swiping his hand down his cheeks to remove the rain trickling through the twelve-hour shadow on his face. "Tell me you got something I can use."

God knew, the last thing he wanted was to interrupt Archer's Monday post-game highlights with a whole lot of zilch.

The medical examiner reached into his jacket pocket and held a clear, plastic evidence bag in Kelly's direction. "Just this business card. She was clutching it in her right hand."

The expensive linen stock was both crumpled and water logged, but the embossed printing was clearly legible. Kelly flipped the card over and back. Only two words were printed on the front—*Dirty Deeds*, along with a Chicago area phone number.

He frowned. Sounded like a Sicilian clean-up crew. "Any idea what this is about?"

DeFranco peered at him over the top of his glasses, unrolling a body bag on Ruby's left. "Um, that's your job?"

Kelly grunted and slapped the evidence bag against his palm. Archer hadn't mentioned Ruby being involved with the mob. Their deal focused more on the local pushers who ran the South Side. He shook his head and turned away, slogging up the slope toward where Ramirez stood watch over the waiting squad.

"Yeah, well, asking questions *is* my job." Starting with the two witnesses who'd found the body. "Let me know as soon as the labs are in."

"I always do."

Kelly smirked, the wet sand dragging at his boots until he'd cleared the beach. A white news van pulled into the parking lot just as he rounded the squad's hood, and he snatched the clipboard Ramirez offered him before quickly ducking into the front passenger seat.

Until he had something to go on, he had no intention of being stopped for a bunch of questions he couldn't answer.

Drying his palms along the thighs of his jeans, he twisted to face the back seat. "Mr. and Mrs...." he flipped through Ramirez's report. "Weaver?"

"Why are we being detained?" Hostility glinted in Mr. Weaver's blue eyes, and he jerked his head toward Ramirez through the side window. "We already told the other officer everything we know." His wife pressed her fingers to her lips, and Mr. Weaver slung an arm around her shoulders, pulling her to his side.

"I just have a few follow-up questions, and then I'll have Officer Ramirez drive you home." Kelly smiled. "Standard procedure, I promise."

Mr. Weaver's thinning hair was plastered to his forehead. His wife's dishwater blonde curls dripped over the collar of her white blouse and light spring jacket. Not standard attire for the weather by a long shot. "Can I ask why you were out walking the beach on a day like this?"

"We weren't." Mr. Weaver snuck a peek at his wife. She shivered and he pulled her in tighter, nodding toward the opposite window. "We live across the street. Clarice and I were having brunch when she looked out the patio doors and noticed..." He swallowed. "Something strange rolling in the waves."

Kelly shifted his focus to Mrs. Weaver's drawn face. "When you first saw the body, did you see anyone else nearby? Anything that looked out of place or even something that seemed normal for the time of day?"

"Of course not." She shuddered a second time and Mr. Weaver reached over with his other hand to squeeze her knee. "I would've told the first officer right away." Peering up at her husband, she shook her head. "Oh, Howard, this is just ghastly. How could something like this happen here?"

Howard Weaver patted his wife's leg, murmuring softly, and Kelly glanced at the forms to confirm Ramirez had jotted down their address and phone number. "Chances are good the actual crime didn't happen in this area, Mrs. Weaver. Keep in mind, tidal currents and wind can play a factor in where the deceased washes up."

She gasped and clapped a hand over her mouth. "Oh, that poor girl."

Yeah, maybe not the best visual to leave them with but, shit. Kelly's senses had hardened over time. An unavoidable hazard of the job. Christ knew, after fifteen years on the force, he'd seen it all.

Still, a little diversion at this junction might go a long way toward making the Weavers more comfortable, just in case he needed them for a later, follow-up visit. "One last thing and then we'll make sure to get you home safe." He held up the business card. "Do either of you recognize this?"

Mrs. Weaver reached for the evidence bag and studied the card a second before shaking her head. She handed it to her husband and his lips firmed. "No."

Kelly hesitated, sliding the bag from Mr. Weaver's fingers. If he trusted anything, it was his gut. His time on the force, coupled with the hell Jaclyn had put him through, made damn sure he could spot a lie fifty miles off. Considering how Mr. Weaver had barely glanced at the evidence, Kelly would place bets he'd just been handed a pile of bullshit. And he would win. "You sure about that, Mr. Weaver?"

"Of course, I'm sure. My wife and I had nothing to do with his heinous crime." He waved his hand around the car. "Now if you're done giving us the third degree, I insist you have someone take us home or I'm calling my attorney."

Kelly nodded, grabbing the door handle. Whatever secrets the guy was hiding, they worried him enough to lawyer up. If he did, the small crack that had just appeared in the case would slam shut. Better to let Mr. Weaver go now and approach him later. After things had settled. Kelly slid his attention to Mrs. Weaver. And when his wife wasn't around. "Thanks very much for your time. I'll be in touch if there's anything else we need."

He stepped into the freezing rain and Ramirez turned as he slammed the door. He jerked his thumb in the Weaver's direction, unzipped his jacket and tucked the clipboard and business card inside. "Take 'em home and have a patrol swing by to make sure everything's quiet."

She nodded as he pivoted toward his car, waving off the slew of reporters that had arrived while he'd been interviewing the Weavers. Once behind the wheel, he cranked the heat, worked the clipboard and evidence bag from his jacket and tossed them to the passenger seat.

He reached inside his breast pocket for his cell. A glance down at the business card, and he thumbed in the number.

Long moments stretched, filled with dead air. A series of clicks like the line was being redirected to a call center in India, and he frowned, checking the screen to make sure he hadn't been disconnected.

The call finally rang through, and he slapped the phone back to his ear. "Password," a male voice answered.

Kelly hesitated. "Uh…"

The line went dead.

He held the phone away from his face, scowling. "Damn, Ruby, what kinda shit mess were you in?"

Another tap of the screen to speed-dial Archer, and Kelly rested his wrist on the steering wheel as he waited for his friend to answer.

"What do you want, asshole? It's my day off."

"Hey, buddy." Kelly dropped his head back to the seat, eyes closed. "I got some bad news."

Meet the Author

Shady Grace makes Northern Ontario her home, where the bush is so thick you can't see two feet past the tree line. Perhaps the mystery of the woods was what initially sparked her need to write. She adores strong alpha males who fall for fiery, independent women, in settings with humorous dialogue and action-filled plots. Shady believes love and sex should be exciting and unforgettable. Being able to write about it is better than cheesecake.

Shady Grace is the new pen name of multi-published erotic author BL Bonita, who earned a starred review from Publishers Weekly for Dark Sun Rising. Visit her website at www.shadygrace.weebly.com, and find her on Facebook at www.facebook.com/shadygraceerotica.

www.ingramcontent.com/pod-product-compliance
Lightning Source LLC
Chambersburg PA
CBHW050751250626
47155CB00005B/2020